HOT MALL SANTA

A GAY HOLIDAY ROMCOM

A.J. TRUMAN

TRUMAN BOOKS

ACKNOWLEDGMENTS

Thank you to PS for your notes and MZ for your ongoing support. Thank you to Bring Design for the cover, and Emma and Lee for blurb notes. And of course, I couldn't have done this without your enthusiasm and encouragement, Outsiders!

What's an Outsider, you say? Oh, just a cool club where you can be the first to know about my new books and receive exclusive content. Join the Outsiders today at www.ajtruman.com/outsiders.

This book is dedicated to everybody in the retail trenches this holiday season. Thank you for helping us find the perfect gifts for loved ones and ourselves, for putting the store back together after we trash it every day, and for answering all of our oddest questions. You are the backbone of the holiday season.

-A.J. (former employee of Pier 1 Imports, Waldenbooks, and Banana Republic)

CHAPTER 1

Five weeks until Christmas

FOR TOM WEBSTER, today was typical for this time of year. In other words, busy. Decades of marketing and commercialization had turned consumers into Shopping Terminators during the holidays, and in retail, "the holiday season" had arrived back in late October.

As The Décor Store's top sales associate, he scrambled around the floor that Monday before Thanksgiving assisting customers looking for the right knickknack and furniture item that would complete their souls—or at least their living rooms.

"Excuse me, what do you think of this end table?" A woman stopped him as he carried an ottoman up to the register for another customer. She stared at the piece of furniture, searching for meaning as if it were a piece of Impressionist art.

"This line is fantastic quality. I love the cherry color of the wood. What color is your couch?"

"Taupe."

"Perfect. That contrast will really make it pop. I've had this end table for years, and it's held up." While that would seem to be an obvious line, it was the truth.

"It would go well, but..." She creased her brow and rubbed her chin. "It seems a little plain, don't you think?"

"Think of it as a blank slate. If you do something like this..." Tom put down the ottoman. He plucked a table lamp from a nearby display and jogged to the back corner for a red-tinted vase. He organized the lamp and vase on the end table. "This adds more color and dimension. What do you think?"

"I love the combination! I'm moving into a townhouse. He got to keep the house in the divorce." For some, this might seem like an overshare, but it was normal for Tom. He had found that for the upper-middle-class wives that spent their weekdays shopping in the Oakville Mall, retail employees like him doubled as therapists and life coaches.

"He may have the house, but you have the style," Tom said.

"You're right." She got choked up for a second. "You're right. I'll take the whole thing," she said, gesturing to the table, lamp, and vase.

Tom leaned in. "If you take the floor model as is, I can try and get you fifteen percent off. Usually, we're only authorized to do ten, but I want you to have a great holiday season in your beautiful new place."

"Thank you so much!" She almost tried to hug him, but stopped herself.

"My pleasure. I just need to talk to my manager."

"You mean you're not the manager? You should be!" she said.

He smiled politely, even if the statement had an unintentional sting.

Tom dropped off the ottoman to the customer waiting by the register and found the store manager in front setting up a new furniture display. He went off a strict layout sent down from corporate.

"Antonio?" Tom's voice shook in his throat. He braced himself for some Antonio smolder that would go straight to his core...and other appendages.

"How's my best employee doing?"

Why Antonio was a store manager at a suburban Décor Store and not on a *Men's Health* cover was beyond Tom.

"Good. I'm good. Doing good."

Ever since Antonio transferred to the store a year and a half ago, Tom was smitten, perpetually thunderstruck by his full lips, crisply ironed shirts, and perfectly styled hair.

"I need manager approval," Tom said. "This woman wants the floor model of the Lorden end table. I was hoping to give her fifteen percent off."

"Is it really scratched up?"

"No. Maybe a small nick on one of the legs." Tom wondered what Antonio's bare legs looked like. Muscular calves with a dusting of hair. The Décor Store had an unfortunate dress code of pants-only, even in the summer. "She's having a rough time. She just got divorced, right before the holidays. Imagine if you and Milo broke up this time to year."

Tom imagined it all the time. And then he imagined comforting Antonio in the stock room and on the table in the break room.

"Not like that would ever happen, but come on, Antonio." Tom gave him his best flirty smile. "It's the holidays. Have a heart."

Antonio smiled back, charmed by Tom's pitch. And maybe more? Tom knew it was pointless to pine for his happily coupled boss, but that smolder...

"Fine," Antonio said, with fake annoyance.

"I think your heart just grew two sizes." And Tom's cock threatened to grow, too.

"Since I have you here, can you work Thanksgiving night?"

Last year, The Décor Store decided to open on Thanksgiving evening rather than wait until Black Friday. Corporate said they wanted to "better accommodate our passionate consumers," but who was so passionate about home furnishings that they had to shop mere hours after the Thanksgiving meal?

Tom mulled the offer. "I'm working every day Thanksgiving weekend, though."

"Charlie asked to switch with somebody. His family decided to go to Michigan for Thanksgiving, and since you stay local, I figured you'd be around. You love working holidays and getting that sweet, sweet time and a half."

Tom didn't love working holidays. But ever since he pulled through in an emergency Memorial Day when three employees "called in sick," he'd been known as the holiday guy. Tom never traveled for the holidays. His parents split when he was five, and even though his dad lived with his new family in Omaha, Tom only saw him when he came up to the Chicagoland area for work. Tom had tried spending Thanksgiving down there when he was eight, but he felt as out of place as a foreign exchange student who didn't speak the language. He spent all his holidays with his mom who also lived in Oakville.

"Please, Tom? It would really help me out if you picked up Charlie's shift."

He couldn't say no to that those lips, eyes, and hair.

"Sure."

"You're the best." Antonio slapped Tom's shoulder, and perhaps it was Tom's lustful imagination, but he thought Antonio's hand lingered for a second longer than necessary.

Tom returned to his customer and delivered the good news.

"Actually, you know what, I don't think I'm going to take it," she said. "It's not speaking to me like I thought it did. But thank you for your help." She gingerly left the store, not realizing or caring that she gave him retail blue balls.

"Great," Tom said to himself.

The woman was almost plowed over as she walked out by Kirsten, Tom's best friend and fellow sales associate. Kirsten ran inside, catching her breath, as if she'd just escaped a robot uprising. Her desperate eyes found Tom.

"Hey," he said to her.

"You're ten minutes late," Antonio said, but Kirsten held up her hand to silence him. She could do that without it coming off as obnoxious. It was a true testament to her personality.

"Tom," she said, still getting her heart rate under control. "You will never..."

"What? What is it?"

"Hot...Mall...Santa."

———

KIRSTEN PULLED Tom to the throw pillow wall in the back corner of the store. She leaned against it, pretending it was a couch, since employees couldn't lounge on actual furniture during store hours. Tom fluffed out the throw pillows and tidied up the wall in case any customers came by.

"What is a Hot Mall Santa?"

"It's pretty self-explanatory. Tom, I've never seen anything like him." Kirsten went on to tell him about her sighting of the Hot Mall Santa. She parked her car, and as she walked into the mall, she saw this guy in a Santa Suit swagger through the front doors. He wore Aviator shades, and his Santa jacket was half-unbuttoned, revealing a sleeveless white undershirt. She demonstrated his pimp stroll. Even through the suit, Kirsten could tell he had an amazing body.

"He was like the living embodiment of sex. His beard was pulled down, and he had these amazing cheeks and jaw. It's like whatever the cheek and jaw equivalent is to an ass you can bounce a quarter off of."

"I think you're imagining things."

"He had a six pack."

Tom motioned for her to keep her voice down. He would tell her they were at work, but that made no difference to Kirsten.

"His pants hung low on his hips. His dick is probably so huge it's pushing them down."

"Kirsten!"

"What? Just stating the facts."

"What happened to the regular mall Santa? The guy who was actually round and jolly?"

"I think he retired. And why have a regular Santa when you can have a hot Santa?"

An old lady wandered into their section. Tom felt his whole face turn red.

"I'm sorry about her. Can I help you find something?" he asked the old lady.

"I saw him, too," she said. "He is quite the stud."

"I told you," Kirsten said.

"His ass looks great in those red pants."

Tom would never look at old ladies the same way again. Kirsten gave the woman a hi-five.

"Whose ass *ever* looks good in Santa pants? I can't wait to sit on his lap," Kirsten said.

"I think you're too old for that," Tom said.

"Me, too!" the old lady said. The women hi-fived again in a ya-ya sisterhood of horniness.

Antonio found them. Kirsten let out a *busted* sigh.

"Tom, I need you up front."

"Sorry," he said.

"Sorry, Antonio," Kirsten said with zero sincerity. "Tom, go with Antonio."

She shot Tom a knowing look, and he signaled to her to knock it off.

————

WHILE TOM HELPED a woman pick out stemware, he pictured what this Hot Mall Santa must look like. He wondered if he was as hot at Kirsten claimed. Her taste in men could be dubious. She still found Johnny Depp attractive, after all.

"You're thinking about him, aren't you?" Kirsten showed up at his side.

The woman viewing stemware cocked an eyebrow at Tom.

"I think I'll take this set." She pointed set to a box of blue-stemmed glasses.

"Great choice! They can ring you up at the register."

"Thanks for shopping at The Décor Store! You have a Décor day!" Kirsten waved at the woman as she walked away. Then back to Tom. "He is seriously so fucking hot."

"You've made your point." Tom checked to make sure Antonio wasn't around.

"Don't worry. Your one true love is on break."

Tom shushed her.

"Don't shush me!"

He tidied up the placemats so their edges were all aligned. It was small details like that that Tom believed helped sales.

"Tom, you need to make like Elsa and let it go."

"There's nothing to let go. I don't care about Antonio."

"Bullshit. Ever since he transferred to our store, you have been hopelessly crushing on him. And I do mean hopeless, because he has a boyfriend."

"I know that." Although there were moments when Tom thought that maybe *just maybe* things weren't so great with Milo, those moments when Antonio was a bit friendlier than usual, like the extra second his hand stayed on his shoulder today.

"I don't think you do. Tom, there are plenty of available men out there. Why do you always fixate on the ones you can't have?"

"The thrill of the chase."

"There's no chase, though." She flipped through stacks of placemats like they were a deck of cards. "And to be QH." That stood for *quite honest*. "He's a d-bag."

"No, he's not! He's smart, caring, and kind!" Tom instantly hung his head. So maybe he did have a crush.

"Yeah, kind of a d-bag. Why hasn't he made you assistant manager yet? You're ridiculously overqualified."

"Maybe I'm not. I'm still learning."

"You've been here for three years. You know merchandise SKUs like they're your social security number. You actually care about these abominations of humanity we call customers. Hell, you should be running this store."

"I spoke to him about it. He said he's going to put my name in for the next assistant manager position that comes up in the region."

"He said that six months ago. He's stringing you along. I don't know why he wouldn't want to make you his ass man."

"What?"

"Assistant Manager." Kirsten chuckled. "I just thought of that."

"Clever," Tom deadpanned.

"But seriously...what gives?"

Frankly, Tom didn't know. He knew he had the right stuff to be management. Regional directors and most corporate leadership started as sales associates. The Décor Store prided itself on promoting from within, which is one reason why he applied to work there. But whenever he tried to talk about it with Antonio, he was blinded by those chestnut eyes. A part of Tom thought that Antonio was afraid to let him go. Assistant managers were assigned to stores that needed them. Maybe he couldn't bear the thought of Tom leaving his store and them not working together. It was a selfish reason, but one that would be motivated by romantic feelings for Tom, which Tom couldn't fault him on.

"Forget about Antonio. Maybe you can have some fun with Hot Mall Santa."

"Hot Mall Santa is probably straight, statistically speaking."

"Excellent." Kirsten rubbed her hands together. "You have to check him out when you go on your lunch break."

"I will." Tom finished fixing up the placemats, despite Kirsten's destructiveness.

"Oh, I see one for me!" Kirsten and Tom made a pact

that whenever a straight male customer came into the store, he would be hers. It happened so infrequently. These men were like deer in the headlights at a store like this, and Kirsten loved to be their guide. "And he's a cute one!" She pulled her top down so her cleavage was on full display.

"Go get 'em."

"Let me know if Hot Mall Santa jingles your bells."

CHAPTER 2

The Oakville Mall had four wings that all connected at the center, where the food court was. Santa's Workshop was set up in the South Wing, where few people ventured. It was like the old section of a town that was booming in the fifties but had gone into decay since. The anchor store was an empty Borders that had yet to be replaced, and other storefronts remained vacant, save for the occasional Halloween pop-up store.

Unlike most patrons, Tom liked coming to the South Wing. He could remember every store that occupied every space over the past decade. It was a time capsule of his childhood, when the South Wing was *the* section of the mall. Back then, he couldn't wait until he was old enough to work at the mall. He felt like the coolest fourth grader when he got to go with his mom on shopping trips. Oh, youth. When working retail seemed like a glamorous career. He applied at every store he could and wound up getting hired part-time at a Talbot's as a sophomore in high school. It seemed he'd always had a knack for serving a clientele of older women. Tom continued working at the mall through college, getting the job at The Décor Store his senior year. He enjoyed being on his feet, having a flexible schedule, and coming into contact with a colorful array of characters.

Santa's Workshop consisted of a snowy path lit by glowing candy canes that led to Santa's throne and behind that, a holiday hut, where he assumed Santa and the elves drank out of flasks. There were no guests in line yet. This time of year was reserved mostly for holiday die-hards and moms who wanted to cross *taking kids to meet Santa* off their list before the crush of the season.

Santa emerged from the hut, and holy holiday hard-on, Kirsten was not lying. The Santa costume could not hide such a specimen of male beauty. Those cheekbones could not be obscured by the fake beard. He slouched in his Santa chair, legs spread, and perhaps Kirsten was right about his dick.

Tom kept walking, keeping it casual, pretending that he totally wasn't checking out Santa Claus. Tom was not a fan of the holiday season. He didn't hate it like others, but the holidays were synonymous with crazy Christmas shoppers, so it wasn't a time of year he looked forward to.

Until now.

He could feel Hot Mall Santa staring at him. Those dark, full eyebrows should come with a warning, and those eyes should wear a condom if they were going to completely penetrate Tom.

"It's closed," Hot Mall Santa said. He had a deep gravelly voice that practically dared Tom to sprout wood.

"What?" Tom asked.

"The Borders is closed."

In his quest to be casual, Tom realized he was headed straight for the empty store.

"Oh," Tom said. "That's a surprise."

"Borders went out of business a few years ago."

"Oh. Right." Tom didn't know why, but he still went up to the store and pulled on the doors, like he had to stay in character for the sake of his pride. The doors were locked. "I guess you're right."

"So, what do you want for Christmas?"

"I'm too old to ask Santa for anything."

Hot Mall Santa patted his lap. What a wonderful lap it was. He must do squats. No, lunges.

"I am definitely too old for that."

"You're never too old for Santa."

"You have real kids to attend to." Tom pointed to the empty line at Santa's Workshop. *Damn.* "Business will pick up after Thanksgiving."

"I could use the practice." Hot Mall Santa patted his lap again. *This guy had to be fucking with me.* He knew that straight guys who weren't openly homophobic all secretly reveled in toying with gay guys.

"I'll pass."

"Anything special you want?"

Dear Santa, all I want for Christmas is you...inside me.

"Nope."

Hot Mall Santa continued probing Tom with those penetrating eyes. "You sure? We all want something."

And actually, Tom gave it some thought. He wanted to wash his feelings for Antonio out of his head. He needed a new crush, someone to pine over that wasn't his boss, someone who could be a real romantic possibility. Tom had never had a serious boyfriend. He kept finding himself drawn to unattainable guys who were either straight or taken. He hoped there was someone out there who could make him feel the way he felt around Antonio, someone who he had a realistic shot of dating.

But until then, there was Hot Mall Santa, a perfect short-term fixation.

"Thanks, Santa."

"You haven't told me what you wanted." His thick eyebrows lifted in curiosity. He was almost too beautiful to look at.

Almost.

"You're Santa. You should know." Tom turned around and headed for the food court.

CHAPTER 3

Four weeks until Christmas

THANKSGIVING WEEKEND WAS PREDICTABLY HECTIC. Tom thought turkey was supposed to make people sleepy, but it only made them hungrier for deals. Black Friday nearly destroyed him. Two co-workers "called out sick," and he was stuck holding down the fort with Eddie, the assistant manager. Tom found himself managing up a lot when he was working with him. Eddie took smoke breaks nearly every hour, never checked other stores if they didn't have something in stock, and for any cash register function the slightest bit complex, he called for Tom.

Fortunately, Kirsten offered to come in. As goofy as she could be, when things got busy, she stepped up and put on her serious employee gameface. Kirsten was a senior in college and planned to leave retail behind when she graduated. They started at The Décor Store the same day. It wasn't until they both discovered their mutual love of the TV show *Broad City*, particularly the classic episode about pegging, that their co-worker relationship gelled into friendship. Tom's closest friends all came from stores in the mall. Retail folk had been in the trenches together.

Tom had Monday and Tuesday off from work after the holiday. He relaxed on his mom's couch and took advantage of her cable TV. He happily got sucked into a seven-hour marathon of *House Hunters*. Even though it was all fake, it still made for good television. When he returned to the mall on Wednesday, he just so happened to park outside the South Wing.

Oops.

It was cold out, so his best option was to walk through the South Wing to get to The Décor Store. And if he happened to check out Hot Mall Santa, then so be it.

He did this every morning and lunch break for the next week. That moment of seeing Hot Mall Santa provided a stronger jolt than his coffee. Whenever he was about to think about Antonio, Hot Mall Santa shoved him out of his mind.

Word about Hot Mall Santa must have spread. The lines for Santa's Workshop went to the edge of the snowy landscape. Women scrounged up any kid they could find to get up close to him. Some women and gay men went solo, hoping for a chance to sit on his lap. The workers dressed as elves, who had mostly been there for ambience, now had the job of crowd control. But no matter how busy he was, Hot Mall Santa nodded his head at Tom each time he passed.

He's toying with me...and I like it.

The quick pinch of attention was enough to make Tom float through the hectic atmosphere of The Décor Store. In the aisles, he heard women talking about Hot Mall Santa with each other, like he was an event to be experienced.

Tom wondered what kind of women he dated. They had to be no less than supermodels. *What do hot people talk about on dates? Or do they just stare at each other?*

"Hey Tom." Antonio came up to him at the cash register with a schedule in hand. "Would you be able to close tonight?"

"Did Arnie call in sick again? Suffering from a case of New-*Star-Wars*-Movie-Itis?"

"No, it's for me." Antonio tipped his head and parted his lips slightly, an expression that would usually make Tom insta-swoon, but his mind was still cloudy with his daily head nod from Hot Mall Santa. "Milo's sister is in town for dinner unexpectedly. She loves to surprise us."

"Sure. No problem. Is it me and Eddie then?"

"It's you. Eddie is off today. I think you're capable enough to close the store. You've seen me do it a thousand times, and I know you can handle it."

"Doesn't a manager have to be here to close?"

"I can give you my keys. I know you can do this. It'll really demonstrate your management potential."

Tom could close the store with his eyes shut. He had spent years aiding managers in the process, helping them count the money, fill out bank deposit slips, and do a final walkthrough of the store. He was excited for the opportunity.

"Thank you so much." Antonio put a hand on his shoulder, which went straight to Tom's Christmas tree. "I owe you one."

———

THE NEXT DAY, Kirsten came into work with a story to tell. She sat on the part of the counter that held the tissue wrapping paper and sipped her iced coffee.

"I met Hot Mall Santa," she said with absolute seriousness.

Tom wanted her to keep going. He didn't even tell her that employees weren't allowed to be eating or drinking while on the floor.

"Go on," he said.

Kirsten hopped off the wrapping station and paced behind the register. "I said to myself enough was enough. If other adults could sit on his lap, then so could I! So I got to the mall early and waited an hour in line."

"An hour?" That was the kind of wait to ride a ride at an amusement park, not a mall Santa.

"I busied myself listening to *Savage Love* podcasts. I learned some really great tips for giving a hand job. It's all about positioning your elbow."

Tom stopped her from demonstrating and made sure no customers were around. There weren't. It seemed Kirsten was more careful than he gave her credit for.

"BTW, I was not the only childless person on that line. Lots of ladies and gay men."

"Really?"

Kirsten heaved out a dramatic breath, one filled with painful longing. "Tom, he is ridiculously hot. Up close, he is even more attractive. Like The David statue, although I bet he has a much bigger—hi, ma'am. Is that all for you today?" Kirsten took a gravy dish from a lady and rang her up. "Are you a member of our rewards program? If you sign up today, you'll get ten percent off your purchase."

The lady's cheeks were red with second-hand embarrassment. Tom's probably were, too. She shook her head no to the rewards program.

Kirsten finished completing the transaction and wished

the woman a Décor Store Day, which was not an official company line no matter how hard Kirsten tried to make it one.

"I think The David is a grower, not a shower. Anyway," Kirsten said. "It was my turn finally."

"Did you sit on his lap?"

"Fuck to the yes. I sat on his lap and kinda swished around." Kirsten demonstrated, moving her hips and butt, receiving odd looks from nearby customers. "I told him I was trying to get comfortable."

"You gave him a lap dance," Tom said.

"Huh. I guess I did."

"And did he...respond?" Tom was more curious than he should've been. His inner fantasy world hoped that those daily head nods were something more.

"Ugh, no. Not from what I could tell. Those Santa pants must be thicker than we think."

"What did he say?"

"He stuck to the script. He asked me if I was good girl this year. I told him no." Kirsten bit her lip. "I asked what Santa does to bad girls."

"This sounds like a bad porno."

"It was a legitimate inquiry. He said bad girls don't get any gifts. He said I should work on being a good person blah blah blah." Kirsten rolled the cash register stapler in tissue paper. "And that was it."

It sounded anti-climactic to Tom. He had had more of a conversation with Hot Mall Santa without having to stand in line.

"What was he like?" Tom asked.

"Personality-wise? I don't know. Who cares? He's hot. That's his personality."

CHAPTER 4

As someone who'd practically grown up in this mall, Tom loved discovering its secrets. There existed nooks and crannies that he'd found during late nights and lots of time wandering around. About a year ago, he found a door next to where the telephone booths used to be, back when that was a thing. Behind it were stairs that led up to an empty office that overlooked the center of the mall and food court through a two-way mirror. Tom surmised that this was where security used to watch over the mall before the advent of closed-circuit cameras.

Tom loved watching people flit around beneath him, going about their lives oblivious that someone saw them. Kind of like God himself. He looked forward to lunches up here, where he could have peace and quiet.

But today, when Tom came up here, he was not alone. Someone else had discovered his secret spot. Someone wearing an all-red suit.

Alert! Alert! We have a Hot Mall Santa in our midst!

Hot Mall Santa sat in the office chair eating a burger

from Wendy's with one hand and sipping pop with the other. He looked out the two-way mirror, probably playing the God game himself. Tom's chest clamped up with nerves. He turned to leave silently, but the office door creaked. Hot Mall Santa spun around.

"Hey." His beard was pulled down to his neck and his jacket was open, revealing a white tank top that barely contained his pecs and abs. Seeing his face unadorned, Hot Mall Santa looked to be in his early twenties, just like Tom.

"Hey," Tom managed to say, although it was quite the herculean feat on his part.

"Is it okay if I'm here?"

"Probably not." Tom gripped his Chipotle burrito in his hand, and it made him think of other phallic objects.

"Well, I won't tell if you won't." Hot Mall Santa pointed to the extra chair against the wall. He made space on the desk where his Wendy's bag was.

"Thanks." Tom was too nervous to eat in front of him. "How did you find this place?"

"I was headed to the food court, and this pack of moms was coming at me, so I ran into the first door I saw, which led me here." Hot Mall Santa took fries out of his Wendy's bag and dipped them in ketchup. "Am I hogging your space?"

"No. It's not my space."

"But I take it you've been up here before."

"Yeah. I like coming up here. It's quiet. I like looking at the bustle, not being in it." Tom nudged his chin at the window.

"So you're more of a voyeur."

Tom felt his face get redder than Hot Mall Santa's suit.

"I wouldn't say that." He got too much pleasure from

watching Hot Mall Santa's lips curl around the straw and sip pop.

He checked the clock on the wall. He didn't have much time to eat. He couldn't waste precious minutes looking for a new location. And he didn't want to. Tom sat down. He couldn't believe he was in the presence of the one and only Hot Mall Santa.

"So how do you like it here?" Tom asked. "You're quite popular."

"It's the holidays."

"It's not just that."

Hot Mall Santa shrugged modestly. The suggestion seemed to pain him just a bit. "Whatcha reading?"

He pointed at the book Tom carried under his burrito.

"It's all about the best beaches in the U.S."

"You didn't just Google it?"

"I like reading books, not listicles."

Hot Mall Santa signaled for him to pass it over. He studied the cover and flipped through the pages.

Tom unwrapped his burrito. He hoped he didn't look too suggestive eating it in front of him. He doubted Hot Mall Santa would even make that connection.

"What's your favorite beach?" Hot Mall Santa asked.

"Miami. Venice Beach and Santa Monica in California look like a lot of fun, but apparently the Pacific Ocean doesn't warm up like the Atlantic. The water in Florida is said to be warmest. The water on the Gulf side is warmer, but after that oil spill disaster, I don't trust being in there."

"The Atlantic is just as polluted."

"But it has better waves," Tom said. "At least that's what I've read."

Hot Mall Santa handed back the book. He picked another fry out from his bag. "Don't you love the smell?

That's my favorite part of the ocean. They should bottle it up and sell that shit."

"The Décor Store has ocean-scented candles."

"It's not the same." Hot Mall Santa slouched in the office chair like he did on his Santa Throne. He had this aura of cool. Tom believed some people were born with it, and others were meant to be fidgety, neurotic messes. "You know that salty smell," he said.

"I don't. I've never been to the beach."

"To any beach?" Hot Mall Santa asked.

"My family and I would go to Lake Michigan every summer."

"That doesn't count."

"I know. I hate when people here say they're going to the beach. You're not! You're going to a lake with tiny waves, imported sand, and no salt water." Tom and Hot Mall Santa shared a laugh. "I want to dip my feet in the ocean one day. Miami, Venice Beach. I'll even take the Jersey shore."

"They're all great."

"You've been?" Tom asked. As if Hot Mall Santa wasn't already sexy and naturally cool. He'd been everywhere Tom wanted to go.

"Venice is pretty crunchy. Lots of tattoo parlors, and the scent of weed hangs in the air. Also, you can go into the ocean anywhere in California. Just pull off to the side of the road. But in Jersey, you have to pay to go on the beach. They have boardwalks, though. And Miami's just a constant party, especially South Beach. People will party till dawn then sleep on the sand."

"You really have been everywhere. Why are you here in Oakville, Illinois then?"

Hot Mall Santa seemed to consider this seriously, but

then a smiled cracked on his face. "I'm a sucker for the holidays. I've always wanted to experience a white Christmas."

"I'll remember you said that when it dips below freezing in a few weeks." Tom ate his burrito extra slow. He wasn't going to make a scene in front of His Hotness.

"So when is your beach vacation?" Hot Mall Santa asked.

"I don't know. Whenever I can save up the money. I'm taking my mom and me." Tom flushed with embarrassment. A vacation with his mother? It sounded like a beach-set sequel to *Psycho*. "She's never been either. It's a special occasion kind of thing. I don't hang out all the time with my mom. I have friends."

I have friends? That is literally the lamest thing that has ever been said!

But Hot Mall Santa didn't flinch. "I hope you two get to go. If you go to Miami, try to stay as close to Ocean Drive as you can. It has great restaurants and clubs. And the best people watching ever."

"Better than the Oakville Mall?"

"Hmmm...it's a close race." Hot Mall Santa took another fry from his Wendy's bag. "You want one?"

"You don't take your fries out of the bag?" Tom asked. *And you eat deep-fried carbohydrates and still look like that?*

"No. I've always liked eating them like this. The bag keeps in the heat."

"Keeps them from getting cold."

"Yeah."

"I love the fries that fall out of the carton into the bottom of the bag. They're like..."

"Bonus fries," Hot Mall Santa said, basically reading Tom's mind. He pinned Tom down with his eyes. They had a ring of amber around the edges, as if they were two solar eclipses.

Tom remembered to chew his fry with his mouth closed.

Hot Mall Santa sipped the last of his pop and gathered up his trash. "My fans are waiting for me," he said mockingly. "Thanks for letting me share your secret lunch spot."

He left Tom to finish his burrito alone, but Tom couldn't eat. Not when his mouth wouldn't stop smiling.

CHAPTER 5

The rest of the day passed without issue. Customers seemed to be on their best, non-cuckoo behavior, as if they sensed that Tom was busy thinking about his lunch with Hot Mall Santa. He pictured Hot Mall Santa shoving him up against the two-way mirror and kissing him, then clearing away his Wendy's to take Tom on the desk.

He was allowed to fantasize. That was what Hot Mall Santa was for.

At six o'clock, most of the day employees left, and the night shift came in. The night shifters consisted mostly of people who worked a regular nine-to-five job. Kirsten took her coat and purse from her locker in the break room. Tom considered telling her about his lunch with Hot Mall Santa. It was something meant to be shared, but he couldn't bring himself to do it. He didn't know why. It didn't feel right to him, like it would sully the good conversation they had.

"Are you working tomorrow?" Kirsten asked.

"No. I'm off. You?"

"Same. I have finals this week. Then I'm all yours." She

threw on her jacket, something cute and frilly that could not handle any temperature under forty degrees.

They walked back onto the floor. Milo waited by the front door, near the main Christmas display of plates and napkins. He looked extra pale and extra short whenever he stood next to Antonio, and Tom supposed they made a cute couple, in an opposites-attract way.

Antonio wore his peacoat as he went over orders by the cash register. The lapels framed his face just right. His eyes lit up when he saw Tom.

"Thank you again for closing," Antonio said. "I won't let it go unnoticed."

"Would you be willing to swear to that statement in court or in front of Décor Store bigwigs?" Kirsten asked.

Tom elbowed her in the side.

"Hey guys!" Milo came over and instantly nestled into Antonio's embrace. If Tom wasn't hopelessly crushing on Antonio, he might've found them to be adorable.

Kirsten shot Tom a stealth eye-roll.

"How's the holiday rush so far?" Milo asked.

"Not bad," Tom said. "Still girding my loins though."

"My friend at Toys 'R' Us said that two dads got into a fist fight over a *Cars* camping set. Some stores have all the fun," Kirsten said.

"At my last store, two women almost got into it over a trivet. I separated them just in time," Antonio said, laughing at the memory.

He had a great laugh. It filled up his whole glorious chest and made his teeth shine brightly in his full mouth.

"What's a trivet, babe?" Milo asked.

Tom didn't look her way, but he knew Kirsten had another eye-roll reserved for *babe*. She made life bearable.

"It's a plate you put under a hot serving dish so you don't damage your table," Tom said.

"And that was worth fighting over?" Milo asked.

"I guess," Tom said.

"Speaking of something to fight over..." Kirsten's eyes bugged out, and Tom followed her stare. "He's here."

Hot Mall Santa spun the ornament display in the front of the store.

"That's your mall's Santa?" Milo asked. "Damn."

"I don't get the hype," Antonio said. "He's not that attractive."

"Oh, come on, babe."

"I don't get it." Antonio narrowed his eyes at Hot Mall Santa for a second before they flicked to Tom, perhaps judging if Tom was as smitten.

"Hey." Hot Mall Santa waved to Tom, sending a ginormous spotlight shining on his face.

"Hey," Tom said, feeling the heat of his co-workers' looks.

"So this is where you work?"

"Yeah."

"Cool."

Other customers stopped what they were doing and joined in staring at this piece of beauty in their presence. Hot Mall Santa acted like none of them existed, like he and Tom were in a play, and the show had to go on.

"Which ornament should I get?" Hot Mall Santa spun the display. "I don't want a glass one because I'll break it."

"You can hang me on your tree," Kirsten said under her breath.

"I like the wooden one of the giftbox." Tom picked out the ornament for him. It was painted blue with a red bow. "It's simple. Not overtly Christmas."

"Just slyly references it and goes about its day."

"Yeah." *Am I smiling like a complete doofus?* Tom caught his reflection in a wreath-framed mirror. *Yep.*

"Okay then." Hot Mall Santa lifted the giftbox ornament off the display. "I don't like when everything is red and green. I prefer some variety with my Christmas decorations. Where do I pay?"

"I can ring you up here." Tom motioned for him to come around to the cash register. He could feel the stares of his co-workers. He wrapped the ornament in tissue paper and placed it in a small paper bag.

"I forgot to mention at lunch, but if you do go to Miami, check out this restaurant called The News Café. It's got a great view of the ocean."

"Thanks. I will."

Hot Mall Santa gave him a five dollar bill, and Tom made the appropriate change. He looked in the bag at his wrapped-up ornament. "Sweet. Have a good night." Hot Mall Santa waved at Antonio, Kirsten, and Milo. "Great store you got here."

Tom couldn't help but notice the hard expression creasing Antonio's face as he watched Hot Mall Santa leave.

"Damn," Milo said again.

"We should go. We don't want to be late," Antonio said. He maneuvered Milo to the door. "Night."

They exited in the opposite direction of Hot Mall Santa.

Kirsten's face stared at Tom, full of shock and awe. "Lunch?"

"We didn't have lunch together. We just happened to be eating in the same location."

Kirsten nodded, but something told Tom she didn't believe him at all.

CHAPTER 6

The Décor Store got busier as the week went on. The good thing with busy days was that Tom's shift went by in a blink. It was the slow periods where he wanted to gouge his eyes out. Tom didn't see Hot Mall Santa for the next few days. He parked outside the North Wing to get to the store faster. Things were so busy that he ran to the food court for lunch and ate in the break room, where seasonal employees kept interrupting him to ask questions. By the time they figured out how to do their job competently, they'd be gone, so it was kind of a waste.

"I saw your BFF. He's just as busy," Kirsten said to him during one break room lunch. "The line is almost to the Old Navy."

Tom wondered how exhausting it was being Santa. On the one hand, the guy got to sit all day. But he had to talk to kids, which was like its own foreign language.

By Saturday night, Tom needed a drink. He worked a twelve-hour shift because someone "called in sick," but he didn't care how tired he was. He needed a drink. Kirsten wasn't available because she was at a classmate's party, and it was just as well. Tom wanted to be alone. He didn't have the energy to handle her energy.

After closing with Antonio, who didn't ask him anything about Hot Mall Santa, Tom drove to the one gay bar in the area, The Wounded Soldier, which Tom learned through Googling was an expression for an alcoholic drink abandoned by its owner. It also stood for the metaphor of gay Americans who fought and gave their lives for equal rights, according to an old patron who Tom had met one night. The bar, like a troll, sat on a dirt road under a one-lane bridge on the edge of town. The Wounded Soldier had been here for decades, a relic of when gays had to live in the shadows. About five years ago, two wealthy gay men from Chicago who wanted to get away from the busy city life purchased The Wounded Soldier and gave it a complete renovation. Now, it only *looked* old and rundown, as part of its aesthetic. Inside were shiny new booths, a sleek juke box, and an extensive craft beer selection.

Tom ordered a beer and took a seat on a barstool closest to the back. The drink soothed his body after a strenuous week. He was too tired to make conversation, and if he needed anything else, there was always Grindr. A small dance space had been carved out near the jukebox. Some eighties song played. Tom recognized it from the soundtrack at The Décor Store, a song that Tom had heard approximately ten million times.

"Is this seat taken?"

Tom shook his head no without turning around. He spotted bright red pants and black boots from the corner of his eye.

"Hey." Hot Mall Santa gave him a head nod. His Santa jacket was unbuttoned, and he wore another one of his white tank tops underneath.

"What are you doing here?" Tom asked.

"Grabbing a drink." Hot Mall Santa flagged down the bartender. "What are you drinking?"

"It's called a Daisy Cutter. It's brewed by Half-Acre in Chicago."

"I'll take one of those," he said to the bartender.

Tom was going to ask Hot Mall Santa what he was doing here again, as in *Did you know you are at a gay bar?* But he put two and two together. Tom hated when people asked him if he was gay. He just wanted them to know. And there was no way a guy makes the trek to The Wounded Soldier just for the beer selection.

Hot Mall Santa's fake beard was pulled down to his neck. His cheekbones were a study in geometric precision, and his light stubble alone nearly set Tom on fire. "I like it," he said of the beer. "Good call."

"Yeah." Tom couldn't believe it. Hot Mall Santa was sitting next to him at a gay bar! Hot Gay Mall Santa was more like it. "How'd you find this place?"

"Google."

"Right."

"Do you ever wonder how guys found bars like these before the Internet?" Hot Mall Santa asked.

"Word of mouth, I guess."

"But you had to be careful to ask the right people."

Guys openly checked out Hot Mall Santa. One asked if he could sit on his lap. Tom wanted to shove the guy away, but to his credit, Hot Mall Santa declined more politely.

"I'm off the clock," he said. "But I'll be at the Oakville Mall tomorrow."

The guy seemed like he would actually be there.

"I'm sorry you have to do deal with that," Tom said.

"He's no worse than the moms."

"Have moms sat on your lap at the mall?"

He nodded. A bit of foam hung on his lower lip, and Tom wished he could lick it off. "It's not as bad as it sounds. They don't really say anything. They just get a picture taken for their Facebook feeds."

"That's not so bad."

Hot Mall Santa shrugged. He tapped his finger against his glass. "They just want to look."

He didn't sound flattered, but Tom supposed it got tiring day in and day out.

"My friend Kirsten went to see you."

"I remember. She kind of gave me a lap dance." They both laughed at that.

"She said you were a complete professional because you didn't 'react.'" He said that last word in air quotes. "Now I get why."

"One woman grabbed it outright while her three kids waited by the elves."

"Are you serious? You could get her arrested for that."

He raised his eyebrows in doubt. "'Mall Santa Sexually Harassed' is a headline most people would laugh at."

Tom didn't want to admit he was right. "I guess it's cool that so many people want to see you."

"I guess."

"There's nothing wrong with people thinking you're good looking."

"It's weird when all people do is compliment something about you that you had no part in. It's not like being praised for something I've done or made. Just something I am. Like a zoo animal."

Tom didn't know what it felt like to be wanted like that, to be lusted after. He always thought guys like Hot Mall Santa had it made, especially in the gay community. Hell, even now, there were a few pairs of eyes checking him out, while Tom was glossed over. But he saw for the first time that perhaps being the center of attention came with its own perils. He wasn't sure what exactly the downsides were to being beautiful, but judging by Hot Mall Santa's expression, they did exist.

"Let me get the next round," Tom said.

"I won't stop you."

"By the way, I'm Tom." He held out his hand.

"Randall."

They shook. Hot Mall Santa—er, Randall—had a firm grip.

———

SOME TIME LATER, they sat across from each other in one of the booths against the wall. Tom cut himself off after the second beer so that he could drive home, but Randall moved onto his third. The alcohol had worn off Randall's cool, Hot Mall Santa varnish and turned him into an animated storyteller.

"He enlisted to fight in the Civil War at age forty, where he was shot in the arm, the knee, and the chest, but he still survived and went on to become president. Rutherford B. Hayes was a badass."

"I've never seen someone so passionate about our fifteenth president."

"Nineteenth," Randall said in between beer sips. "There's this whole period of one-term presidents people have forgotten about."

For the past twenty minutes, Randall had regaled Tom with random facts about past presidents. Apparently the grandsons of John Tyler, our tenth president, were still alive.

"Have you always been such a history buff?" Tom asked.

"No. To be honest, I never paid too much attention in school. On long car trips though, listening to music gets boring fast. So then I moved onto podcasts, and I listened to one about crazy facts of American history. Then I picked up an audiobook on George Washington, and it turned into this thing where I'm making my way through all the U.S. presidents. Hayes was tough because there aren't a lot of biographies on him, unfairly so."

"Isn't it weird when you find yourself wanting to learn things you had no interest in at school? Last year, I found myself re-reading *To Kill A Mockingbird* for fun."

"There's this adult part of my brain that's like 'knowledge is cool,'" Randall said in a robot voice.

"Is your brain a machine?"

"I have no idea why I did that voice. I like to think that my brain speaks in a British accent."

Tom broke into a loud, hyena-like laugh that didn't feel embarrassing in the moment. Probably because Randall's laugh, more like a guffaw, was just as silly. They attracted odd looks. *You guys wish you were having as much fun as us!*

Randall picked a piece of lint off his coat's faux-fur trim.

"Why are you still in your Santa costume?"

"I came from work. I really needed a drink and to not be around kids."

They clinked their glasses to that. The beer matched the ring of amber in his irises. Tom figured he shouldn't be studying his eyes so much.

"Your co-workers seem cool. I didn't mean to embarrass you the other night," Randall said.

"We weren't expecting a celebrity to walk into our store."

Speaking of co-workers, Tom's heart clenched up when he thought he saw Antonio come into The Wounded

Soldier. He didn't know why, but being around Randall and Antonio at the same time sent his awkward meter off the charts.

"Do you see someone?" Randall peered at the front entrance. Even the way his hazel eyes squinted and lips parted slightly was like he was forever posing for a magazine cover.

The guy walked up to the bar, and phew. Not Antonio.

"I just thought that was my boss."

"Oh, he does kind of look like the guy I saw the other night, the one with the blond husband."

"Boyfriend," Tom said quickly. "Boyfriend. They're just boyfriends."

Randall cocked an eyebrow.

"They are! Why are you looking at me that way?"

"In what way?"

"In that way with your eyebrows and your eyes and your mouth."

"Those are parts of my face."

"You know what I mean."

He seesawed his head and gave it a second of thought. Tom could watch him make any facial expression.

"You don't seem that enthralled with the idea of your boss being married."

There was no use lying to Randall. He felt he could trust him, if only because he didn't talk to anyone Tom knew. "I might have a slight crush on him." Tom put his head on the table. "I can't believe I just said that. I'm such a cliché."

"I'm sure you're not the only one."

"Thus the cliché part." Hearing him say it out loud make Tom realize how pathetic pining for someone he couldn't have was. It was like still believing in the Tooth Fairy. Or Santa Claus.

"What am I doing? It's so dumb. He has a boyfriend. They will probably get married."

"Probably."

"You think so?"

Randall held up his hands in defense. "I'm just going off of your information."

"You're right. Now I get why they're called crushes. They crush you," Tom said. He watched couples dance to the jukebox music. What did they know that he didn't? "What about you? Any boyfriends?"

"Nope," he said proudly. "I like having the freedom to do what I want, go where I want. I have a goal to visit all fifty states."

Tom raised his glass. "Welcome to the Land of Lincoln."

"And besides, people just wind up letting you down anyway," he said, with a sudden edge to his voice. "Like with your crush, you only see your boss as this perfect guy, but if you were to actually date him, you'd find his flaws. You'd see he wasn't so perfect."

"We all have flaws. Well, except for you." Tom reached over and took off his Santa hat, revealing thick brown hair that any comb would get a boner going through. Even after being under a hat all day, it still maintained its volume and shine.

"Oh! I know this song!" Randall put back on his hat and got out of the booth. "Will you dance with me?"

"I don't dance."

"It's the song from *Footloose*. It would go against the message of the movie if you *didn't* dance." His large hand remained extended. It could not be refused.

Tom joined him in the dance space. He felt eyes on him, wondering how the hell he got so lucky. Randall had this natural cool aura to him so that even though his moves weren't different from what others were doing, he came off like the best dancer in there.

Tom watched his body turn and spin. He glimpsed the tight ass inside those unflattering red pants. But he found himself coming back to the goofy smile on his face. That was the most interesting part of him in the moment, the one that put Tom at ease and made him let go of his inhibitions.

He danced with just as much abandon as the Hot Mall Santa across from him. For the rest of that song, Tom didn't care who was watching or what they thought. Especially himself. He most definitely cut loose. Footloose.

The next song that came on was *Baby, It's Cold Outside*.

"Finally, an actual holiday song," Randall said.

The dance space cleared up. Tom went back to their booth.

"Where are you going?"

"Someone ended the dance party."

"Not so." Randall's large hand beckoned him again.

Is he really asking me to slow dance? Are we at senior prom?

Tom thought it was a joke at first, but his hand didn't move.

He rejoined Randall on the dance floor, and they slow danced together, their chests not an inch apart. Soon, other couples joined them, taking one spotlight off Tom. But a stronger one remained.

Randall kept looking at Tom. His eyes were lethal weapons that could get Tom to do anything in the moment. He licked his full lips, and Tom had to make sure he wasn't dancing too close or else there'd be a poking situation.

"You're still in your Santa suit," Tom said.

"I know."

"People are probably wondering what you're doing in a Santa Suit here."

"So let them wonder." Randall leaned in for a kiss.

Tom got to feel and taste those full, warm lips himself. It was like a door to a new world. Narnia maybe, if he'd read those books. Randall pulled away, but Tom wanted more. He had just gotten a hit of the best drug on the planet, and he was having instant withdrawal.

"What are you doing after this?" Tom asked him.

"Dunno."

"Do you want to come back to my place and watch a movie?" Tom chided himself for such a hackneyed line.

Hot Mall Santa rubbed circles on Tom's hand with his thumb. "Only if it's a Christmas movie."

CHAPTER 7

Hot Mall Santa is in my car.

Tom played it cool as best he could. He wasn't some innocent virgin looking to have his first experience and gee whizzing into his pants. He'd been around the block his fair share. But never with a guy as good looking as Randall. He had the face and the body, and also the personality, too. Despite feeling awkward and inadequate, he'd had fun talking and dancing with him. Tom had fantasized about guys like him. Fantasies weren't supposed to come true.

They were tonight.

Unless he really did just want to watch a Christmas movie.

"Where do you live?" Tom asked.

"I'm on the other side of town, by the highway."

"That's not too far from the mall."

Randall gazed out the window at beautiful Oakville with its suburban townhouse developments and ample retail chains.

"I'll bet you can't wait to go to the next state."

"Illinois has its charms."

At a red light, Tom glanced at Randall in the passenger seat. The sly smile on his face nearly ripped the clothes off Tom's back.

We're so not watching a movie.

————

"THIS IS YOUR FAVORITE CHRISTMAS MOVIE?" He pointed at Tom's TV. It was a large screen he'd gotten on the one Black Friday he ever had off. The TV was the nicest thing in his one-bedroom apartment, with the rest made up of used furniture, discounted Décor Store merchandise, and things his mom had given him. Tom's uncle owned the apartment complex and let him live here for free. Without that, he'd still be living at home. The assistant manager promotion, and the pay bump it would provide, could not come fast enough.

"Yes. It's a classic."

"*Die Hard* is not a Christmas movie." Randall shook his head at the screen.

"It is! It takes place on Christmas Eve."

"That's only a coincidence."

Tom actually gave this serious thought on the car ride back to his apartment. Many of his favorite Christmas movies like *Home Alone* and *The Santa Clause* starred little kids, and he didn't want to get it on with a guy while children ran amok on screen. He didn't want to put on a comedy like *Elf* because he didn't want Randall laughing and breaking the moment. And if he put on *The Family Stone*, he'd instantly get sucked in and forget about the guy on his couch. Deciding which movie to put on kept him calm in the car and restricted his cock from getting even harder.

"It's a great movie," Tom said, though he wasn't the

biggest fan of it. Yet it was perfect for playing in the background. And young Bruce Willis wasn't bad to look at. Neither was old Bruce Willis, to be QH, as Kirsten would say.

Randall plopped down on the couch with his legs spread. Tom couldn't tell if he was hard. Even though they kissed in the bar, it was still a possibility that he actually wanted to watch a movie.

"Do you want anything to drink?" Tom asked.

"I'll take another beer."

Tom pulled two bottles of the Half-Acre Daisy Cutter from his fridge. Now that he was home, he could drink again, and he needed to. He took a gulp before he left his kitchen.

"Thanks." Randall took his beer.

Tom sat beside him and played the movie. Any fears and doubts he had about this night vanished the second John McClane got inside Argyle's limo. That was when Hot Mall Santa put his arm around Tom. By the time McClane arrived at Nakatomi Plaza, their tongues were in each other's mouths.

I am making out with Hot Mall Santa. I might get to see Hot Mall Santa naked.

Tom melted to his touch, though not to the cheap material of the Santa suit that rubbed against his cheek. He thought the Oakville Mall would've sprung for a better quality costume. They had a Neiman Marcus, after all.

Tom was ready for any and everything. When you had the opportunity to hook up with a guy like this, you made the most of it because you didn't know when or if the gods would ever be this kind to you again. He grabbed at Randall's faux fur-trimmed lapels and pulled him closer, shoving his tongue into his pretty, Hot Mall Santa mouth. His hands traveled across his chest and tumbled down his washboard ads. Tom had thought that washboard abs were something that only existed in cologne ads. Speaking of cologne, Randall smelled fantastic. A dash of cologne, but mostly some natural sexy man scent that was pure pheromones. *Hot Mall Santa Sweat, the new fragrance by Calvin Klein.*

He surprised Tom with tender kisses. He pressed against Tom's lips then cheeks then neck. It was almost intimate.

"You're really fucking sexy," Randall said.

Me? Have you seen yourself? Tom would've said the same thing back to him, but sexy couldn't be used to describe Hot Mall Santa, not when it'd just been used to describe a mere mortal like himself.

Tom racked his brain for an appropriate compliment. "You're super-duper fucking sexy."

Super-duper fucking sexy? Not his finest moment.

Tom distracted from his subpar wordplay by straddling Randall. He felt something hard brushing against his most sensitive area. God, he wanted it so bad. He wanted to savor every inch of this man's body like it was Godiva chocolate. Tom grinded against the hardness. *This is how you give a fucking lap dance, Kirsten.* Randall let out a deep moan that vibrated in Tom's mouth. He grabbed Tom's hair and held his mouth in place for very non-tender kisses. Tom grazed his fingers over his scruffy cheekbones, then his ear lobes. Yes, even the man's ears managed to be super-duper fucking sexy.

"Yeah," Randall whispered out in his deep voice. Tom grinded against him, letting his thick erection put pressure on his ass.

Tom pushed at his Santa jacket, and Randall whipped it off without taking his lips off Tom. Tom felt the rope-like cords of his muscles and shoulders. He could've bench-pressed all eight reindeer at once. Tom couldn't wait to get manhandled by those arms. He reached under his sleeveless undershirt, and he could hear the angels sing out. That chest. Those abs. No fabric between them anymore. Tom could feel all the heat his muscles had to offer.

In the background, Alan Rickman said something smarmy. Without detaching himself from the hottest of mall Santas, Tom reached for the remote on the couch arm and turned off the TV.

"I think movie time is over," Tom said. "Spoiler alert: Bruce Willis saves the day."

"Which way is your bedroom?"

"That way." Tom pointed to the hall. It was a one-bedroom apartment, so it wasn't like he had to give turn-by-turn directions.

Randall lifted both of them up and carried Tom to the bedroom. He threw him down on the bed, which thankfully, Tom had made before leaving for work. That didn't always happen. He couldn't excuse the rest of the mess in his room, but it wasn't like Randall was looking. His dark eyes were fixed solely on Tom.

Tom leaned across the bed to reach into his nightstand. He took out condoms and an extra-large bottle of lube he got the one time he borrowed his mom's Costco card. It was the more economically prudent option.

"I have my own condoms," Randall said, standing over the bed.

"Oh, *excuse* me."

"I have to use magnums." He took out his wallet and removed one such prophylactic.

"Okay." Tom stifled a laugh. He'd heard that line from guys before. It was never true. "Sure."

Randall dropped his Santa pants in one fluid motion

and his jumbo-sized cock shot up in the air, like a middle finger to Tom. Like a whole bunch of middle fingers. It was just as long as it was thick.

Holy shit. Tom wasn't sure a magnum would do the trick.

"You literally have a North Pole in your pants."

"Thanks?"

Tom didn't want to blink. He didn't want it to go away. He knew it was going to hurt, but dammit, pain was gain. He curled a finger to get Randall to come closer. Tom crawled across his made bed and put that submarine of a cock into his mouth. It stretched his jaw, but was totally worth it. He loved the feeling of this warm, throbbing thickness filling up his mouth.

Randall let out strangled moans above him. Tom took that dick as far as he could. He savored the salty taste and musky smell of his balls. He held onto his strong thighs for balance. He thought Randall was pushing his face down, but there was no pressure. The guy ran his hands through Tom's hair, massaging his scalp. It felt really nice, like tender kisses with his fingers.

Tis was not the season for tenderness, though.

Tom went harder on his cock, gagging as he took more of him in his mouth. He could barely wrap a hand around it. He licked the underside of the shaft and tongued his balls.

"Want to try something?" Tom asked.

Randall quirked an eyebrow in rabid curiosity.

Tom lay on his back with his head just off the bed and neck tilted at an angle. Randall lowered his body. He slid part of his cock slowly into Tom's mouth. He cried out in pleasure, a helpless sound that was music to Tom's ears.

Randall fucked his cock in and out of Tom's mouth. Tom was grateful he was up for experimentation. He didn't know if this night would ever happen again, and he didn't care if it broke him. He wanted to be owned by Hot Mall Santa.

"Fuck. Tom. Shit," he said in short gasps as he fucked Tom's face. He bent over Tom to get a deeper angle. Tom slapped his ass and let a finger hover over his hole, which elicited another helpless sound.

Tom coughed when he went a little too far. He wasn't able to take all of Hot Mall Santa. Yet.

"Sorry," Randall said.

"I'm fine." Tom found it sweet that he apologized.

"This is so fucking hot. I could come right now."

"Don't," Tom warned.

"I can't wait to fuck your tight little ass."

Tom's cock ached against his jeans. If he was better coordinated, he would rub himself. His dick yearned to be touched and grabbed.

Randall lifted his cock and let Tom lick his heavy balls. Tom wanted anything he had to offer. Tom's tongue lingered past them and flicked along his taint. Their non-verbal communication was on point because Randall put a leg on the bed, giving Tom access to his pink hole.

"You like tonguing that ass?"

Tom was too busy to respond, and a thumbs-up seemed inappropriate.

"You like rimming Santa?"

Another thumbs-up worthy comment. Tom spat on his puckered opening. He couldn't get enough of Randall's round, robust bubble butt. He wondered what exercises he did to get it so firm. Lunges. No, squats.

Randall stepped back, and Tom sat up. He got a little dizzy as the blood flowed back to his body. Randall's sleeveless undershirt was pushed up and clinging to his sweaty chest. And his Santa hat was still on, cocked to the side, which made Tom's dick twitch with added horniness.

"So who am I?" Tom asked. "The elf being punished for not hitting toy quota? Mrs. Claus's slutty surgeon brother?"

"Surgeon?"

"What? Just because he's slutty doesn't mean he didn't have time to go to med school."

Randall cracked a hazy smile, which might've been the sexiest thing about him at the moment.

"You're funny," he said. The way he looked at Tom sent a volt of fuzzy electricity through his system. But it was replaced by a glint of lust in his eye. "Now get on all fours. Like a reindeer."

Tom nodded along, his cock twitching. He wanted to take off his pants, but wanted Randall to do it more. He held up a finger. "I know how to make this even better."

He rolled over to the nightstand on the other side of his bed where he kept stuff for work. For the holidays, they made employees wear antlers to up the festive atmosphere. The more festive a store looked, the more inclined people were to buy. Tom took the antlers from the nightstand drawer.

"So which reindeer am I? Rudolph? Actually, saying I'm a reindeer implies bestiality."

"You're not a reindeer. You snuck into Santa's workshop pretending to be a reindeer and got caught. You tried to put Blitzen out of work. Now you have to pay the price." Randall signaled for Tom to lie on his back. Tom silently applauded his creativity and wondered if he did improv on the side.

Randall unbuttoned his jeans. Tom's cock sprung up, which after seeing what Randall was packing made him a bit embarrassed. But the guy seemed to approve. Randall put the antlers on Tom, and he instinctively got on all fours.

Tom wasn't sure he'd ever be able to walk again, but oh well.

Randall got behind him and put his assured hands on Tom's hips. Tom shivered with want as he heard the wrapper rip open on the magnum condom. Well, one stocking was going to be stuffed tonight. His lubed fingers pressed into Tom's hole.

"I'm going to go slow," Randall said.

"Give it to me." Tom was drunk on Hot Mall Santa and damn the hangover tomorrow.

He pressed his lips together and groaned when Randall pushed inside. His firm hands controlled Tom's body as he steered his cock inside. It nearly cracked Tom in half. He thrust steadily and carefully, and Tom appreciated the consideration. Soon, whatever discomfort Tom had by his girth was outweighed by the sheer desire pulsing through him. He wanted to get *fucked* by Hot Mall Santa.

"Harder," Tom said.

I am fucking Hot Mall Santa. I am fucking Hot Mall Santa.

Randall slammed the tight hole with his thunderous cock. Tom watched him dominate and pound into his body through the mirror above the headboard. Randall had a pained, serious expression etched on his face. His lips were flushed and pouted. He had ripped off his tank top, exposing the sweat dripping down his chest and flexed abs. (The hat stayed on, natch.) Randall pulled him closer and barreled inside his wrecked hole.

"Fuck!" Tom yelled out. "Fuck me Santa!"

Randall slapped his ass hard. Then again. He fisted Tom's hair, pulling his head back and, for lack of a better term, fucked the life out of him.

"You going to sneak into Santa's workshop again?" He hissed in Tom's ear.

Tom didn't know what he was talking about, until he remembered the story. *Kudos to him for staying in character.*

"Yes, Santa. Yes I am if it means I can get fucked like this again." Tom didn't know if that was the proper answer, but a hungry grunt from Randall told him otherwise.

"I'll just have to keep punishing you until you learn your lesson." He slapped Tom's ass, and Tom could feel the mark forming. He humped Tom between each word of the next sentence: "Don't. Fuck. With. Santa."

Tom stroked himself. Usually doggie style was a bad position for getting himself off, but Hot Mall Santa's Christmas magic kept him rock hard.

"You sneaky devil," Randall said. He swatted away Tom's hand. He took over jerking off duties. His rough hand on Tom's cock and rough cock in Tom's ass was hurtling Tom to the finish line.

"Fuck. Feels so good," Tom muttered out.

"Who said you could enjoy this? You like making Santa angry?"

"Yes!"

"Are you on the naughty list?"

"I'm so fucking naughty, so check that fucking list twice and teach me my fucking lesson." Tom was usually not one for role-playing, and these lines would make him cringe in the morning, but the holiday spirit had taken hold of him. He knew this was probably his only turn to ride Hot Mall Santa, so he wanted to do it right. Leave nothing on the field, as straight guys loved to say.

Randall's breath lingered on Tom's ear. "Maybe next time, I'll have to tie you up to make sure you don't cause anymore trouble."

Next time? One could hope.

"Ready to get your gingerbread house frosted?" Randall

said to him through the mirror. His hand tightened around Tom's dick.

"Make it a White Christmas, Santa."

Hot Mall Santa fucked him extra hard, in sweaty and desperate thrusts. The sound of his slick skin slapping against Tom echoed against the walls.

"Fuck!" He grunted and emptied himself inside his magnum condom inside Tom's ass. Seconds later, Tom shot his load onto his comforter.

They both collapsed. Tom didn't care that he was in a puddle of his own making. He had Randall's jacked frame covering him like a blanket, and they stayed like that the rest of the night.

Dear Santa, you can come down my chimney anytime you want.

And then a curious thing happened. Randall kissed Tom's shoulder. It was quick, but there was something so inherently intimate and downright sweet about it, which Tom didn't expect after what they just did. He didn't have a Christmas pun to describe it.

CHAPTER 8

Randall left early the next morning and took an Uber back to his place. He had to wash his costume to get rid of any potential love stains, then hightail it to the mall. They had spooned in bed, but that wasn't so atypical. Tom had done that with guys in the past, though usually he lay awake unable to sleep. This time, he was out cold, cocooned in Randall's arms.

Since Tom was working an afternoon shift, he could sleep in. He dreamt of his night with Randall. He wasn't sure if what happened was all a dream.

It was no dream.

I fucked Hot Mall Santa.

Tom woke up feeling like a million bucks. Well, a million bucks and a sore asshole. He could still smell the tangy scent of sex and Randall's musk on his sheets. He sang in the shower and in the car to work. The radio played Paul McCartney's *Wonderful Christmastime*, a holiday song Tom absolutely loathed. It was the root canal of Christmas songs. But Tom couldn't get enough.

"Siiiiiimply haaaaaaving a wonderful Christmastime!" He belted the lyrics out in the car at full volume.

Tom walked into the mall in a full-on post-sex swagger. Jacket slung over his shoulder, sunglasses on, a tricked-out remix of *Wonderful Christmastime* playing in his head. *Look at all these hopeless moms, only shopping at Oakville to get a moment with Hot Mall Santa. If only they knew...*

He didn't enter by the Santa wing. It was too soon to see him. Tom didn't want him to think he was a stalker.

Nothing could shake Tom's swagger. Not even Antonio telling him he had to unload a merchandise truck because one of the stockroom guys called in sick.

"I would have Jessa do it, but she has a bad back," Antonio said.

"It's totally cool." Tom leaned against a column that held a candle endcap display. Unloading the truck would allow him to zone out and think about the amazing night he had.

"I wish I could have you out on the floor," Antonio said. *Hot Mall Santa had me on the bed.* "But trucks don't unload themselves." *Hot Mall Santa unloaded inside me.*

"It's fine. We gotta do what we gotta do," Tom said.

Antonio flashed him a warm smile. "I really appreciate your great attitude."

Tom waved off the compliment. "I'll get to it."

He didn't wait for Antonio to respond. He whooshed through the back door into the stockroom, as if he were floating on a cloud.

———

TOM'S HEART began to speed up as his lunch break neared. Since he worked a later shift, he and Randall wouldn't run into each other in their secret lunch place. But Tom planned to casually stroll by Santa's workshop to catch a glimpse of the man, maybe enjoy a little bit of banter before he left. Also, Tom wouldn't admit it, but he kept thinking about Randall's comment last night about a next time. He held out a sliver of hope that could happen.

"Great job guys!" Antonio said when he came into the stockroom.

With Alex, the stockroom employee who showed up for work, they had unloaded and unpacked a truck of new merchandise, everything from furniture to knickknacks. Nobody knew what would be on trucks. Corporate stocked them. It was their job to unpack and sell. Tom pictured his night with Randall, but after a while, the actual images of fucking gave way to memories of their conversation in the bar, of the goofy way he danced to *Footloose*, of the way he kissed Tom's shoulder after sex. Tom touched his shoulder, like he was trying to feel some of the heat left over from Randall's lips.

"I'm going to take my break," Tom said.

"Thanks again. Good teamwork." Antonio looked at him for an extra second, something Tom couldn't stand around for. He had a guy to casually stroll past.

"See you in thirty," Tom said. He took off his Décor Store apron, put it in his locker, and entered the wild world of the Oakville Mall. The halls were more crowded, filled with determined shoppers rather than strolling, bored, comfortable housewives looking to fritter away an afternoon.

Tom entered the South Wing, which wasn't as clogged as it probably had been during the day. He found himself on the verge of powerwalking, ready to elbow anyone who got in his way. Was he still high on the Hot Mall Santa sex he had last night? Tom thought about his monster cock and if

Randall had ruined him, literally and figuratively, for future men.

Santa's Workshop was still abuzz even though it was after six. Tom checked himself out in the reflection of an empty store window. He looked fine, no different from last night, but he combed his hair with his fingers. He also popped in an Altoid.

Tom hid behind a calendar kiosk. Randall held court on his throne with about half a dozen women and gay men circling him. These weren't the typical suburban moms that had come to see Santa. These people were young and hot. The women had blown out hair and a fresh face of makeup. The gay men wore clinging jeans that showed off more curves than a closed driving course.

And Randall was loving it.

He had one leg swung over the chair arm and was telling them a story. Tom couldn't hear what he was saying, but they were loving it. Every damn word. Guys like Randall were automatically popular. They would always be flocked to and surrounded.

"What am I doing?" Tom mumbled to himself. His hair smelled of cardboard boxes and his baggy jeans were built for comfort not sex appeal. What happened between him and Randall was a fluke. Their relationship was built on Tom being at the right place at the right time. He was someone to talk to in an empty, abandoned office and the only person he knew in a random gay bar. Against real competition, like the sextet flanking the throne, Tom didn't stand a chance.

He walked away, unseen by Randall. He treated himself to a Cinnabon for lunch and made his way to his secret spot. He glanced out at the mall from high on his clandestine perch, and for a second, he felt like a mighty king. Tom tossed his Cinnabon bag on the desk. He spotted something sticking out underneath. The air coming from the heating vent made it flap around.

Tom squatted down and pulled a folded piece of paper taped under the middle drawer.

Thought you might need this before your big trip. Look in the right bottom drawer.

He opened the drawer where a tube of SPF 50 sunscreen and a book *50 Beaches To See Before You Die* waited for him.

Maybe there would be a next time.

CHAPTER 9

Three weeks until Christmas

TOM'S SCHEDULE devolved into a mess, all thanks to Julie Who Cares. That was the name of the character in The Décor Store's national Christmas ad campaign. In each commercial, she went through the store looking for the perfect gift for someone most people would give an envelope of cash to, like a mailman or crossing guard. She wanted to find them the perfect gift because she *cared so much*. The spots went viral, the actress who played Julie was interviewed on *Good Morning America*, and about six people so far had posted Julie memes on Tom's Facebook.

Julie Who Cared was working, which meant business was picking up more than they expected. Little-to-no downtime existed in Tom's shifts. He and Kirsten couldn't hang out on the pillow wall. One day, Antonio ordered in lunch for everyone, which they ate quickly in the break room.

Tom was exhausted and didn't have the energy to elbow his way over to Santa's Workshop, and with the extra crowds, he doubted Randall had any energy himself. He put the book and bottle of sunscreen on his nightstand and might've looked at them before he went to sleep. (And he might've used the sunscreen to masturbate once. It worked surprisingly well.) He figured it was just a nice gesture by Randall, perhaps a thank you for an awesome fuck.

Tom left him a note taped under the desk with a gift in the bottom drawer. *Thank you for the book and sunscreen! Here's something to protect against any more grabby visitors to Santa's Workshop.*

In the drawer, he left an athletic supporter.

Tom worked the closing shift the next day and didn't have his break until eight at night thanks to extended hours. But sometime around six-thirty, he saw a familiar guy in a Santa costume walk past The Décor Store and glance inside. Randall smiled at him briefly and kept walking. A group of girls followed him with their phones out.

When he finally went on break, Tom steadied his breath as he felt under the desk and silently cheered when he pulled down a note.

Please tell Julie Who Cares to relax. Santa's worried about her. She's going to give herself a heart attack picking out the right gift for the captain of her daughter's lacrosse team. Take it from a guy who gives out gifts for a living: you can't please everyone.

P.S. I left something in our drawer that should make this communication much easier.

Inside the bottom drawer, he placed a candy cane pen, Christmas stationary, and a roll of tape. (Not everything had to be holiday-themed!)

Tom reread the note, smiling extra hard at the "our drawer" part.

His shift didn't end until 10:45. The store closed at ten, but it took the rest of the time to clean up the store and get it ready for the next day, when it would be destroyed all over again. He formulated a response to Randall in his head all during clean-up.

When they locked up the store for the night, Tom darted to the secret spot and placed his response. He also left a box of markers, in case either one of them felt inspired to draw.

And so it went like this for the next week. Notes under desks and split-second glances through store windows. Tom printed out an internet article titled *10 Crazy Things You Didn't Know About Rutherford B. Hayes* and stuck it in their drawer. They never thought to ask for each other's phone numbers. Tom liked this way better. He hated waiting for a text or email from someone while on duty. He would check his phone once a minute and time would drag and then when he did receive an answer, it would never live up to the anticipation that had mounted in his head.

"What's gotten into you?" Kirsten asked him, almost one week after Tom and Randall had last seen each other in person. She swept up in kitchenware, and Tom restocked and cleaned up displays.

"What do you mean?"

"It's like you've been in your own world."

In a way, he had. He and Randall lived in this secret world with hidden rooms and coded messages, like they were spies.

"Are you seeing someone?" Kirsten put down her broom.

"No."

"Hooking up with someone?"

"No."

"Rubbing up against someone?"

"No." Tom did his best to hide any trace of lying. He had wanted to tell Kirsten, but he wasn't sure what Randall's closet status was. If she spread the word that the Hot Mall

Santa was gay, or even bi, he might even lose his job. Tom also didn't want it getting back to him that he was blabbing about their hookup. After this week, their hookup didn't feel like just a hookup anymore.

Kirsten studied his face for an extra moment. She could usually squeeze the truth out of him by staring in his eyes and claiming he was lying over and over until he confessed. She should really be a detective, or a kindergarten teacher.

Before she could continue her interrogation, Tom moved to another section to clean up. The store needed it.

———

Tom pretty much stumbled to his car. Working in retail was like picking up after the world's messiest, most inconsiderate roommate. Customers had no concept of putting things back where they came from. They thought just because Tom made an hourly wage, they could leave the store in disarray. All that reaching, squatting, lifting, and carrying turned Tom's muscles to sludge.

He sat in his car for a second before starting the engine. It would all be over soon, he reminded himself. The holiday season was a sprint, not a marathon. *Just make it to January, and then you can collapse.*

While driving out of the mall parking lot, he saw a familiar presence waiting at the bus stop. His red suit glowed under the street lamp. Tom pulled up to the curb.

"What are you doing here?" Tom asked.

"Waiting," Randall said.

Tom didn't realize he took the bus. Most people he worked with drove. Oakville was a town that had a drive-thru everything.

"Where's the bus?" Tom asked.

"You tell me," Randall said. He kept his Santa suit buttoned up to fight against the cold.

"Does it still come this time of night?"

"I hope so." It seemed even Santa's Workshop was staying open later for the holidays. Randall rocked back and forth to stay warm in the bus shelter.

"I can give you a ride home," Tom said.

"Are you sure?"

"Yes." Tom patted the passenger seat head rest, like this was a no-brainer.

"I'm out of the way from your apartment, I think."

"I don't care. You're freezing. Is that suit insulated?"

"Not at all."

"You need to speak to your elves about that." Tom cocked his head. "Get in."

Randall's smile gave Tom a blast of heat stronger than what came through the vent.

Once he got in his car, Randall pulled up turn-by-turn directions on his phone to guide him. Now that they were together, in an enclosed space, a sense of awkwardness over-came Tom. They had joked and talked through notes, but would that translate face-to-face? Tom had met up with guys he chatted with online, where they had great text chemistry, but it fizzled in person.

"Thanks." Randall raked a hand through his hair, which just like at The Wounded Soldier, had not been flattened by his Santa hat.

"Of course. I couldn't let Santa Claus freeze." Tom kept his hands at ten and two. "And thanks for the gifts."

"Likewise. I had no idea Hayes was the first president to use a typewriter! I hope you get to use the sunscreen."

There was something to his voice, like maybe he could be the one who'd rub it on Tom. Or so Tom hoped.

"How's it been for you?" Tom asked. "It seems like Santa's Workshop has been blowing up."

"My boss said it's never been this crowded. My arms and legs are sore from holding kids on my lap."

"And adults," Tom added, thinking of the fans he saw surrounding Hot Mall Santa. "Adults love you."

"Yeah. They do," he said, scuffing up Tom's confidence. "It's kind of weird, though."

"You have Santa groupies."

"Lucky me," he said sarcastically. Tom swooned at his raised eyebrows. "All they do is stare at me and ask about Santa shit."

"Well, you are..." Tom gestured at his Santa suit. "If the hat with the white puffball at the end of it fits..."

"It's like I'm just an exhibit. It gets tiring. That's why I like you. We talk about other stuff."

Did he just say he liked me? Like me in a general, friendly sense, probably. Tom felt his cheeks redden. He was glad that their relationship, whatever it was, wasn't one-sided. He was able to provide something of value to him.

Tom exited the highway and drove into the heart of Beacon Strip. Beacon Strip was a relic of Oakville's industrial past. This manufacturing company Beacon had a pair of mills employing thousands of people, and stores and restaurants had sprung up around it. Once the company went under in the seventies, and residents moved into nicer subdivisions on the mall's side of town, the neighborhood atrophied. Now it was a step above a ghost town, empty storefronts and parking lots with weeds growing in the cracks of the pavement. The only thriving business was a bar, and apparently a motel.

"People actually stay here?" Tom asked when he pulled into the motel's parking lot. All the times he'd seen it from the highway, he thought it was empty and only used for people to cheat on their spouses.

"It's not too bad. Cheap," Randall said.

Tom felt bad that he didn't ask Randall about his living situation the first time they hung out. He assumed he lived in a neighboring suburb, and frankly, he had, um, other things on the brain that night.

The Beacon Strip Motel was a row of rooms, similar to the Bates Motel in Tom's mind.

"It works. I got a warm bed and clean water." Randall shrugged, as if there were nothing else he needed. "I'm only here for a few weeks, and it's just a place to sleep."

Even though he was right, it still felt sad to Tom, the thought of anyone spending the holidays alone in a decrepit motel.

"It's a nice room," he said.

"It is?" Tom and everyone else in town imagined the worst of the Beacon Strip Motel. "How did you find this place?"

"Priceline."

Good for Beacon Strip Motel keeping up with the digital revolution.

"Want to see?"

They got out of the car. A light dusting of snow began to fall from the sky. It was nothing a Midwesterner couldn't handle. Tom doubted it would even stick to the roads. Randall treated it as the most beautiful precipitation he'd ever seen. It was probably his first white Christmas. He held his hands out to touch it, lifted his head, laughed as it dotted his cheeks. Who knew that beneath the raging sex appeal, there would be a layer of dorkiness, and that it could be nothing short of adorable?

"NICE," Tom said. Yes, the comforter was about twenty years out of style, but the room had all the furnishings of any other hotel room. It even had a small flat-screen TV sitting on the dresser.

What caught Tom's eye wasn't the décor but the string of Christmas lights taped around the perimeter, where the wall met the ceiling. Randall kept the overhead light off and just turned on his Christmas lights, giving the room a glint of magic.

"Wow," Tom said. "Did you put those up?"

He nodded yes, proud of his design. "It makes the room a lot more festive."

The only decoration in Tom's apartment was a fake Christmas tree that his mom had decorated with plastic ornaments and lights. "You have to have *something*. It's the holidays," she'd told him. Being surrounded by the holidays during the day was enough for him.

Tom clocked the gift box ornament hanging from one of the light strings. The sight made his cheeks get warm.

"I didn't think you'd be so into Christmas," Tom said. "You have to listen to people ask you for gifts all day long when the holidays should really be about giving. I've had customers scream at me because we were out of holiday stemware and how were they going to throw Christmas dinner now?"

Randall took off his Santa jacket, revealing another white sleeveless shirt underneath, and those familiar muscles bulging out.

"I love the holidays. All of it." He sat on the edge of the bed.

Tom looked at him in disbelief. He leaned against the

dresser, unsure whether he had the green light to join Randall.

"You're not sick of it?" Tom asked.

"No. I guess I'm making up for lost time."

"Lost time? You didn't celebrate Christmas enough as a kid?"

"More like never. I grew up as a Jehovah's Witnesses. We didn't celebrate any holidays, because most of them have pagan roots. My parents would take me out of school whenever there was any kind of holiday celebration. And I mean any. We're talking Valentine's Day-levels here."

"So you never got a Valentine's card in school?"

He shook his head no. As trifling and forgettable as they were, Tom couldn't imagine missing out. He held onto the Valentine's Day card his (obviously straight) elementary school crush gave him—the same obligatory card that he gave every kid in class—for years. The card was addressed to a Tim, not Tom, but he cherished it just as hard.

Randall's mouth stretched wide in a glorious smile. "I remember my mother covering my ears when we'd be in the store so I wouldn't hear the holiday music."

"It is pretty bad." The Décor Store played an endless loop of Christmas music that by mid-December made Tom want to bury his head in the pillow wall.

"I was punished for a month for turning our living room plant into a Christmas tree, and another month for lighting firecrackers on the Fourth of July. After they caught me jerking off to a department store catalogue, the men's swimwear page, they warned me every single day that homosexuals do not inherit God's kingdom."

Tom put his hand on his heart.

"Not all Jehovah's Witnesses are like that. I still talk to an aunt and cousin of mine. My parents are just run-of-the-mill homophobes on top of being devout believers."

Even though Randall told this story with a smile, there was hurt behind those eyes.

"Once I turned eighteen, I left and never looked back. I wanted to go places and celebrate things. I took odd jobs where I could find them. When I saw a listing for the Oakville Mall Santa, it felt meant to be."

"So that's why you travel so much." Tom sat next to him on the bed. Not because he was beckoned or because this seemed like the right moment, but because he didn't want Randall to be alone.

"I'm tired of it, to be honest." His shoulders hunched over. "I've been traveling to different states for over three years now."

"Staying in motels?"

He nodded yes.

"It's like I'm looking for something, but I don't know what it is, and I'm afraid I'll never know what it is, and I'll just pass it by..." He looked down and shook his head. His face glowed in different colors from the lights above. "I get a bit of inspiration from our former presidents. Some of them were just as lost at our age."

"It's not just them. It's all of us." Tom rubbed his back. "We're all figuring it out. You have to give yourself some credit that you'll know what you want when you find it."

"You seem like you have it together." Randall lay back on the bed. Tom joined him. They rested on their sides and faced each other. No touching, but still incredibly intimate.

"I'm good at faking. Let's see...I've been stuck in the same job for three years, and I don't know when I'll ever get promoted. But I keep waiting around..." Tom realized how sad that sounded. Why was he hanging all his hopes on becoming a manager? Whenever Kirsten or his mom suggested he look elsewhere, Tom's stomach tightened up with nerves. He didn't want to look for another path. He preferred to avoid risk. "But I keep waiting around because I'm scared."

He didn't mean to say it aloud, but he knew that in this room, under these twinkling lights, he could say anything.

"And because I'm hopelessly in love with my boss who's taken and definitely not interested." Tom rubbed a hand over his face. Antonio was never going to leave Milo for him. "I've been playing the same game since forever. Crush on guys I have zero chance with. Although somehow I got lucky with you."

Randall looked at him in surprise. Tom smacked a hand over his mouth. He might as well tell him his social security number at this point.

"You have a crush on me?"

"I...I have this condition where I sometimes say things without thinking. Like a lot."

"Tourette's?"

"Not Tourette's. I don't actually have Tourette's. Just plain ole fashioned idiocy."

"You're not an idiot." Randall took Tom's hand off his face. He smoothed his thumb over Tom's fingers, then planted a soft kiss on his middle knuckle.

He inched closer to Tom, his pupils wide and earnest.

"Wait, do you have a crush on me?" Tom asked.

Randall answered with a kiss on the lips.

CHAPTER 10

Two weeks until Christmas

TOM WOKE up the next morning in Randall's arms, fully clothed on top of the motel bed. Bright sun dulled the colorful lights above them. There had been no sex, just a bunch of making out. Like the exact opposite of what had happened a week ago.

And it was wonderful. Their tongues flicked around in each other's mouths and Randall's strong hands ran up and down his frame like he was clay on a potter's wheel. After a while, it stopped and transitioned to holding each other and basking in the glow of the Christmas lights. Tom drifted off into one of the best sleeps of his life, even with the light snoring of Hot Mall Santa in the background.

"Morning," Randall said with a squinty smile. He blocked the sunlight with his hand. How was it possible that he was this sexy just waking up? He had the same messy hair, the same rumpled clothes as Tom, but Randall looked he was posing for a cologne ad and Tom looked like he crawled out of a dumpster.

Tom checked the time on the clock. 7:30. He didn't have to be in until two.

"Do you have to get ready?" Tom asked him.

"Probably." Randall sat up and wiped sleep out of his eyes.

Was last night a fluke? It didn't feel like one. As much as Tom second-guessed himself, he knew that something had shifted between them. They had talked and shared. Randall was sweet and thoughtful and so much more wonderful than the one-dimensional sex object of Tom's fantasies.

"Do you want to grab breakfast?" Tom asked.

Randall whipped off his shirt, exposing his achingly perfect chest. Some people were born lucky, that was it, though Tom realized how dumb that sounded. He might have a dream body, but his home life had been a nightmare.

"We can go out for something quick, like Dunkin Donuts."

"The motel has continental breakfast."

"Continental breakfast?" Tom asked dubiously.

Randall dropped his pants and underwear, revealing his big, swinging dick.

"I can give you some privacy." Tom looked away and crossed his legs to hide the boner springing to life.

"Why? Nothing here you haven't already seen."

Tom took that as permission to look. It would be rude of him not to look, like he was rejecting Randall's body or something. So he soaked in the view, which only lasted a few seconds before Randall wrapped himself in a towel.

"So what does this continental breakfast have?"

"Not much. A muffin tray, coffee. Oh, and a waffle maker."

"What?" Tom stood up. "A waffle maker?"

Tom might've been in love with waffles. There was something about them. They were light, fluffy, syrupy. They were breakfast food, dessert food, and could double as a pillow they were that soft.

"Are you okay?" Randall asked.

"We'll stay here for breakfast," Tom said calmly.

"You're funny. Sexy and funny. You don't see that very often." Randall came over and planted a sweet kiss that had hints of lust.

"You're not so bad yourself, Santa."

————

AFTER BREAKFAST, Tom dropped Randall off at work. He went back to his apartment to shower and get dressed. He watched TV, but his mind kept drifting off to the man behind Hot Mall Santa. He thought about their conversation, about the excitement in his voice when he shared presidential trivia, about his quest to find his calling. And that silly guffaw laugh. Like a Transformer action figure Tom had watched two moms wrestle over in the wee hours of Black Friday years ago, there was more to Randall than met the eye.

Tom went to work a little early so that he could make a cameo at Santa's Workshop. He had to park in the back rows of the massive parking lot. He thought he might hit 10,000 steps on his Fitbit walking from his car to the mall. When he got to the South Wing, a security guard stopped him.

"Are you shopping or visiting Santa?" she asked in an authoritarian voice that matched her black-and-grey uniform.

"Santa?" Tom said meekly.

"You need to get a ticket." She pointed to the kiosk just off to her right, which had once sold cell phone cases, but was now repurposed into a Santa's Workshop admission station.

"Do I have to pay to see Santa?" Tom asked.

"No, it's still free, but now you have to sign up for a time. It's gotten very crowded, and it's about to get even more packed after the story," the woman said.

"What story?"

———

"He's going to be on the news?" Kirsten yelled for the whole Décor Store to hear, even though they were in the break room. She nearly knocked over her Snapple. Tom kept it from falling off the table.

"That's what the woman told me. WACL is doing a report on Oakville Mall's sexy new Santa for the six o'clock news." Randall's presence had gone viral. People posted pictures online, tweeted about him, and news spread. The mall knew the WACL story would be the tipping point. Crowds would become tidal waves of people. It sent a knot of stress tangling in his chest and stomach.

"So Hot Mall Santa is going to be a full-fledged celebrity?" she asked.

"I guess so."

"Who knew Oakville Mall would become famous for something other than the guy who drove his car through the Aeropostale?"

Tom pushed Kirsten's feet off the extra chair and sat down.

"This is awesome," she said. "You seem stressed."

"I do?"

"Yeah. Your shift hasn't started yet." She leaned forward and put her hands on his shoulders. "It's going to be okay. The store will be extra packed thanks to Hot Mall Santa and Julie Who Cares, but in two weeks, it will all be over."

Tom nodded, letting her think that's what actually bothered him. He doubted Randall would want anything to do with him now that he was going to be famous. He was Tom's celebrity crush, and celebrity crushes never worked out. Save for Hugh Grant in *Notting Hill*.

She offered him some of her Oven-Baked Lay's. He politely declined.

"Can you imagine all the people who will be hitting on Hot Mall Santa?" she said with a far-off look. "There will be ladies and gay guys who will be giving him actual lap dances and slipping him their number. Depressed, rich housewives will offer him thousands of dollars to have sex. It's going to be insane."

"Insane," Tom repeated, with a hole gnawing inside him.

"Unless he has a girlfriend. Did he mention anything to you about dating someone?"

"No," he said and left it at that.

"All these hot guys usually have a girlfriend. Their high school sweetheart or someone like that. And they're all beautiful and blonde."

Tom picked at his dirty blond hair.

Kirsten took a bite of her orange chicken from Panda Express. She and Tom had a deal in place that come January, they would bring in healthy lunches for work. They did it every year and never made it past the tenth.

"Although I feel bad for whoever she is."

"His girlfriend?" Tom asked. "Possible girlfriend."

Kirsten nodded yes. "Poor girl. Always looking over her shoulder, so to speak. When your boyfriend is that hot and the whole world wants to bang him, how can you ever really trust him?"

Tom's hand dove into her bag of Lay's and grabbed a fistful of potato chips. He crammed them in his mouth. Crumbs tumbled onto his Décor Store apron.

"Cheer up, Tom! I'm sure Hot Mall Santa would be gay for pay."

"Maybe." He held back further commentary.

———

TOM WENT to his car for his second fifteen-minute break later that evening. He needed to feel the fresh, chilly air on his face. He needed to get away from the chaos of the mall. He walked by a TV news van parked on the curb and people fawning over a real-life TV news van at the Oakville Mall.

He reached his car, parked at the edge of the parking lot, not too far from the bus stop was where he'd picked up Randall. Twenty-four hours ago. A simpler time.

"Hey, Tom!" Randall jogged over to his car. Tom immediately looked around to make sure he wasn't being followed with reporters and screaming fans.

"Hey."

"What a crazy day," Randall said with incredible understatement. He pulled down his fake beard, and his smile warmed Tom right up.

"I thought getting interviewed for the six o'clock news and becoming a viral sensation was standard territory for mall Santas."

"If it was, I was lied to during the job interview."

Tom kept looking back at the mall, like it was magnet pulling them to opposite wings.

"I had no idea any of that was happening," Randall said.

"It's exciting. I'm happy for you. You should enjoy it."

"I don't know what I did to earn it."

"You're a sexy Santa."

Randall shrugged his shoulder, unimpressed. Tom could see that he didn't want that to be his only distinguishing characteristic. And after their talk last night, Tom knew that wasn't true, that there was so much inner life underneath that body. Everything Randall had shared made him even sexier in Tom's eyes.

"Can we sit in your car?" Randall shivered in his Santa suit. He still had not thought to wear a real coat to work.

They got inside Tom's car. Randall checked in the rear windshield to make sure the bus wasn't coming yet. He still had a few minutes.

"Are you leaving?"

"I'm on a fifteen-minute break," Tom said. "I have to be back at the Décor Store in seven minutes."

"Then I don't have much time. I just wanted to say that I really enjoyed last night." Randall said. His smile creasing his rugged face was enough to get Tom hard.

"Me, too."

"Maybe we can hang out again sometime before I go."

Before I go. He was moving on, off to another job in another state where he'd be ogled and where he'd find some quiet guy to have fun with. Tom had to keep reminding himself of that.

"How much time do we have?" Randall asked.

"Six minutes. More like two minutes since I have to get back inside."

Randall's hand grazed over Tom's tented pants. He looked at Tom with an *are you thinking what I'm thinking* expression.

"I don't know," Tom said.

"It's worth a shot." Randall kissed him hard, deep. They were making up for their chaste night, and Tom could never resist those big hands and firm lips taking control of his body.

In precious seconds, Randall was unzipping Tom's pants and taking his hard cock in his warm mouth.

"Fuck," Tom gasped out. He glanced out both front windows to make sure no shoppers were coming up.

Randall took him to the base. His warm, full lips sucked his dick. His Santa Hat bobbed up and down. Tom jutted his hips up, and Randall managed to tap a slicked-up finger on his ass. Tom had to give him credit for being so efficient.

"Yes. Yes," Tom whispered. He stopped playing lookout. His eyes could no longer focus.

He filled Randall's mouth with come with four seconds left to spare.

Tom sprinted through the parking lot and got into The Décor Store exactly as his break ended. He put on his apron and immediately stepped behind the register to ring up a growing line of customers. He wondered when he and Randall would see each other next. Randall was leaving in two weeks, onto his next adventure, and like Kirsten said, Tom had to make the most of this small but distinct window of opportunity. He just had to make sure that these pesky feelings brewing inside him stayed locked up. This was Christmas, not Valentine's Day. The holiday was about indulging yourself and doing things you'll regret in January.

CHAPTER 11

Closing and opening back-to-back was never easy. Tom didn't get out of work until eleven last night, and today he had to be there at eight-thirty to open. He picked up the largest cup of coffee Dunkin Donuts was legally allowed to sell him and sipped it in the car. There was already a line out the front doors at South Wing to see Santa. He glared at the men and women in line, most of them without children. They were keeping actual kids from meeting Santa. Why did they have to lose their minds over the one guy who wanted to hang out and have sex with Tom?

Can't you people just watch porn?!

Between the Santa creepers, as Tom called them, and the new Décor Store Julie fanatics, the morning flew by for Tom. He barely had a second to catch his breath. Antonio milled about the store before eventually taking lead on the register when things got busy.

"Do you have any of these extra candle sconces in the back?" An older woman in a pink parka asked Tom.

"We do not. What's on our floor is what we have for candle holders and sconces."

"Hmmm. How many people would you say have touched these sconces?"

"I...I don't know." Tom thought he'd heard every question in the book from customers, but every single day, they continued to surprise him with a new humdinger.

"Ballpark estimate. How many people, employees and customers, do you think have touched them? I don't like buying things that are covered in germs."

"You can clean it. There are cleaning instructions on the tag."

"You should really be selling these in boxes, not loose for anyone to leave their DNA on."

Tom didn't know why, but his mind instantly went to somebody jizzing on the sconce. "You can order the sconce online. It'll be shipped in a box. It's free shipping over fifty dollars."

She narrowed her eyes at him. "Well, you just have an answer for everything, don't you?" And then she left.

Just another day in retail.

The pink parka lady stopped just before the store detectors and gawked at Randall, who was coming in. Dressed in his Santa costume, he would've elicited stares normally, but this being the Hot Mall Santa, it was like time stopped.

He came up to Tom.

"Hey, wanted to say hi." Randall looked around and smiled awkwardly at the gawking customers. "Are you free for dinner Thursday night?"

That was two days away and a mental check of his schedule showed Tom he was off by eight that night.

"Sure."

"Cool." He slipped Tom a note with his phone number. "It's crazy in here, so I'll let you get back to work."

"Cool," Tom said, still focused on the audience they had.

"Merry Christmas to all!" Randall yelled out to the onlookers in a great Santa impression as he left.

———

FOR LUNCH, Tom got a Subway sandwich. He figured he should have something moderately healthy to make it through the extra busy season. He also ordered a large fries from Wendy's and kept them in the bag. He had switched breaks with another co-worker so that it lined up with Randall's break. He couldn't wait to surprise him at their secret rendezvous office.

But Randall was not alone.

The office had at least a dozen people in there, all mall employees. Tom read their nametags. There were employees from The Gap, Nordstrom's, Bath and Body Works, the full gamut. Guys and gals. And Randall was the center, sitting on the desk, the star atop of this tree.

They looked up at him, blushing, fawning. Randall pulled a French fry from his Wendy's bag and ate it. Tom hid the bag he brought for him.

"I had this woman sit on my lap and ask for a new husband. Her husband was waiting for her in line and heard every word. Awkward!"

The room echoed with laughter.

"That is amazing. You should write a book or something," the Bath and Body Works person said. His hand grazed Randall's knee. *Fucking Bath and Body Works.*

"Have people outright asked you for sex?" A female Banana Republic sales associate asked.

"They actually installed a guard so if someone does, they are removed immediately. But then that brings up people asking in more creative ways, talking a lot about milk and cookies and how I can enter their fireplaces."

They were eating this up. Tom felt invisible in this room. *Their* room. Randall soaked in the attention. He could talk about the supposed burden of being so attractive as much as he wanted, but he sure knew how to wield that power when he wanted. He didn't seem ashamed.

"Hey," Randall said when his eyes found Tom.

Tom gave a half-wave. He knew he had no claim over Randall, but something about this felt like a violation.

Randall pointed to Tom. "Tom works at the Décor Store."

Everyone said hello back. Tom recognized a bunch of them from his time in the mall. The Bath and Body Works guy gave him a split-second glare before breaking into a fake-friendly smile.

"I was just regaling them with stories from my time in the Santa trenches."

"It's quite an experience," a girl with both eyebrows pierced said. He recognized her from Hot Topic. "Did anyone ever propose to you?"

The group whipped their attention away from Tom and to the guy they were all there to see. Randall did not disappoint. He brought story after story. Tom wished he could go back to pining from afar. He threw out his fries without anyone seeing.

———

DURING A BRIEF LULL in the busyness, after the midday rush and before the after-work crunch, Tom swept up behind the cash register. Ripped tissue paper, unwanted receipts, and ripped-off tags littered the floor. He had stayed and listened to Randall's stories for the rest of the break, but he felt like a groupie. Maybe that was all he was to Randall, his number-one fan. His Christmastime Penny Lane.

Antonio came up to Tom with a clipboard. That meant scheduling changes were afoot.

"Great job today!" Antonio said. Tom wondered if he had tailored his apron so that it tightened at his chest at the right points. "This time of year feels like living inside a tornado."

"Actually, the inside a tornado is calm, according to this special I watched on The Weather Channel."

"Oh."

Tom didn't know why he broke out useless trivia at inopportune times. He could be a conversational party pooper. "But yeah, it's a shit show."

"Question for you. Are you available to work Christmas Eve? I know, you worked Thanksgiving, and I was supposed to give you a break."

"I worked Christmas Eve last year."

"I know, believe me. But a lot of people have put in time-off requests, and the seasonal workers who haven't will probably flake out. I wouldn't be asking you if I didn't need you." Antonio twisted his face as he braced for Tom's answer. "I would owe you."

"You still owe me from Thanksgiving."

"I *double* owe you. Please, Tom." He placed a hand on Tom's shoulder and opened his eyes extra-wide, like he was Puss in Boots from *Shrek*.

They were only open until six on Christmas Eve, and Tom wasn't going anywhere, just his mom's apartment to watch *It's a Wonderful Life*, so it wasn't a huge imposition. Just the principle of the thing. He wished that all this owing could amount to something, like a promotion.

"Fine."

Antonio clapped with graciousness. "You are the best. I will definitely let corporate know about this."

"Thanks, Antonio."

He marked his clipboard, then put it down. He inched closer to Tom and checked to make sure no customers were around. "So, what's going on with you and the mall Santa?"

Hello, left field.

"What?"

"I saw him come in here today to talk to you again. Are you guys friends, or..."

Tom's eyes nearly fell out of his skull.

"I kind of got this feeling he played for our team. Well, Milo thought so after meeting him."

Tom felt exposed, but at the same time, was grateful to have someone else know.

"We've become friends." He could call them friends. That wasn't an exaggeration. Perhaps a stretch of the truth, or even an understatement depending on how one looked at it.

"Well, just be careful," Antonio said. Tom couldn't tell what was going on behind his eyes.

"Careful?"

"That Santa guy seems like a player. I don't trust him."

Had they met the same mall Santa? Tom hadn't heard Antonio be this serious with an issue that didn't involve stealing.

"He's a nice guy," Tom said.

"He seems that way, but I don't want you to be taken advantage of. He just comes in here and is a big celebrity, and everyone is in love with him. That can go to a guy's head, and people can become disposable to him. I just...I don't want to see you get hurt."

Tom's cheeks got warm. He wasn't used to this kind of attention from Antonio of all people. Where was this concern about Tom's schedule? He admitted he liked it, knowing that Antonio cared about him like this.

"You're too good of a guy to fall prey to a person like that."

"He's not...I appreciate the concern, but there's nothing to worry about."

"I can't help but worry about guys I...work with." Antonio put his hand on Tom's shoulder, but it felt totally different this time. Everything did.

"Thanks."

Antonio went back into his office. For the last moments before the after-work crunch of businesspeople grabbing gifts for co-workers and loved ones, Tom remained fixed at the cash register, thinking. Maybe Antonio was right about Randall. The attention could easily go to his head, and there could be ten different Toms out there. Being that beautiful of a specimen was like having a superpower, and all superheroes struggled with using their powers for good. With chiseled abs comes great responsibility, right?

CHAPTER 12

Even though he had his phone number, Tom couldn't work up the nerve to call or text Randall. Antonio's words of warning embedded themselves in his brain.

Tom worked his shift on Thursday and didn't say a word about Randall to Antonio or Kirsten or anyone who dared tried to ask him. He kept to himself, helped customers, and tried not to think about the Hot Mall Santa putting his mind through the wringer.

"Jesus, some woman I was helping with ottoman cushions would not shut up to me about her pap smear." Kirsten took off her apron and tossed it in her locker. Tom stood next to her and folded his up neatly.

"What's a pap smear?" Tom asked.

"It's like a really invasive throat culture, and I'll let you Google the rest." Kirsten shut her locker. "You ready to go?"

Tom put his apron away. He hadn't heard from Randall all day today or yesterday. He'd probably forgotten about him.

"Yeah."

"Cool. Then let's get the F outta here." Kirsten led the way through the store.

Waiting up front, in non-Santa clothes, was Randall. He wore a cable-knit sweater and jeans with scuffed-up non-Santa boots.

"Hey," Randall said. "Are we still on for dinner?"

Tom put his hand on his chest in disbelief. Kirsten was silently having an aneurysm.

"Yeah." Tom looked at Kirsten, who was now blush central. "Yeah."

"Is tonight still good?" Randall asked.

"It is," Kirsten said. She gave Tom a friendly shove forward.

"I'm sorry I didn't call," Tom said.

"It's okay. I told you I'd meet you after work on Thursday."

"Right." Tom tried not to stare, but Randall in normal clothes made Tom's stomach and heart do a trapeze act together. "You look nice."

"The temperature dropped into the twenties, so walking outside in that Santa suit wouldn't cut it anymore."

"Right." Any trepidation Tom had about Randall's multiple boyfriends and fuckbuddies evaporated as if it were 120 degrees outside.

"Shall we?" Randall gestured to the door. "Good seeing you again, Kirsten."

"You, too." She smiled knowingly at Tom before they walked out.

"Where do you want to go to dinner?" Tom asked. "There's an Applebee's not too far from here."

"Do they do take out?" Randall asked. He hunched his hands in his pockets. He still didn't have a coat.

"Even better. They have Carside to Go. You order on your phone, and they bring it out to your car."

"Perfect."

Tom gave him a quizzical look. "We're eating in the car?"

"Yes, but it's going to be worth it. Just trust me." Randall threaded his fingers through Tom's. It was going to be a good night.

―――――

THERE ARE no mountains in Illinois. It is one of the flattest states in the country, and Oakville is frustratingly level. The only change in elevation comes from highway overpasses or when a real estate developer artificially creates hills to build fancy houses on.

It was the latter where Randall had Tom drive them. He would rub Tom's leg whenever he gave him another direction. The car smelled of Randall's woodsy cologne and greasy Applebee's burgers.

"I didn't tell those people about our secret office," Randall said. Tom loved that he called it theirs. "They followed me when I went on break."

"You have fans."

"They feel more like stalkers." Randall turned to look out the windshield. "I'm sorry the secret is out."

"It's okay. It was bound to happen." Tom glanced at him quickly. Randall told him to turn left at the light. "Speaking of, um, secrets and outs...are you, um..."

"I don't bring it up at work. I don't think my boss or the mall would like it for business reasons. But I am to people who care to know the real me."

"I like the real you." He wanted to keep peeling back the beautiful exterior of this dream guy. It was his looks that pulled Tom in originally, but he found that discovering the real Randall was what kept him coming back for more.

Randall had Tom turn right into Veronese Estates, a tony housing development located on a manmade hill at the edges of town. The nicest complexes in the area were all named after artists from the Renaissance, which immediately made them sound cosmopolitan and classy. Gated communities weren't a thing around here, letting Tom drive in unobstructed.

"Did all your mall Santa-ing allow you to buy one of these mansions?" Tom asked.

"Not quite. Keep driving." A smile escaped from the edges of Randall's mouth. It sent a rush of fuzzy warmth through Tom.

Tom drove down the main road, Caravaggio Boulevard, which was lined with McMansions all modeled after Italian villas, with three-car garages natch. Detailed Christmas light arrangements swaddled the exteriors of many of the houses. Tom could've turned off his car's lights and seen perfectly it was that bright.

"I should've brought sunglasses," he said.

"It gets better," Randall said. "Keep driving."

The further they got up the hill, the more elaborate the decorations. Larger-than-life Santa and reindeer depictions on the roof, choreographed twinkling lights.

"There's a neighborhood competition that they take very seriously," Randall said.

"How do you know all this?"

"I overheard some of the moms in line talking about it, and then one of my elf co-workers told me about this place, that I had to see it."

Tom had lived in Oakville his whole life and had never been to Veronese Estates.

"It's..."

"It's over-the-top," Randall said. "Really tacky. That's part of the fun."

"Yeah." These displays were monuments to conspicuous consumption. The artists of the Renaissance must be turning in their graves knowing their names are being associated with these bourgeois-on-steroids neighborhoods.

Tom drove to the top of the hill, which actually got high up. He parked at the end of the cul-de-sac where the road ended. The only houses up here were two that were under construction. By the looks of their wood frames, they were going to be the biggest ones in the development.

From this point, they had a view of the whole development and the swaths of flat, empty land outside Veronese. A warm, Christmas glow emanated from the houses beneath them, followed by instant darkness of the outside world. There was something quaint about the view, like they were inside of those Christmas villages people set up in their homes.

"This is really cool," Tom said.

"The elves did not do this place justice."

Randall took out their to-go boxes, Tom turned on the radio, and they enjoyed their dinner under the stars and above the lights. Randall picked Tom's brain on his family's traditions for each holiday. Tom asked him about funny stories from his travels across the U.S. and his opinion on whether Abraham Lincoln really was gay. ("Most likely. James Buchanan was definitely a big ole queen.") After they finished eating, they continued talking and held hands on the middle console. Tom would make any bargain with the universe for control of the space-time continuum so that this night never would end.

Soon, the talking petered out. They looked out the

window at the stillness of the night and let the soft notes of the radio fill the space. Tom put his head on Randall's shoulder. Tom had been on dates before, but they had never flowed so effortlessly like tonight.

"Where are you going next?" Tom asked.

"I don't know. I have the motel room through the first week of January. Maybe Wisconsin."

Tom heart's felt a jab of pain at the mention of Randall crossing state lines, probably never to return.

"I kind of don't want to leave, you know? I like it here." Randall's heartbeat vibrated against Tom's head.

"You're the star of Oakville."

"That's not why I like it here so much."

Tom could feel everything in Randall's body. All the nerves, all the tensing, all the heart.

"I like you," Randall said. The words hung in the air.

He was leaving. He was wanted by everyone in the Chicagoland area. He could have lovers in other states. Those were just excuses, Tom realized. It was scarier to admit the truth.

"I like you, too."

Randall held him closer. Tom tipped his head up to glance in those gleaming eyes. He lifted himself to kiss Randall, soft kisses like the tender ones Randall gave him their first night together. They made out in his car. It all felt innocent, like they were a pair of 1950s teens at Lover's Lane or something.

But it didn't stay innocent for long. Want and need overtook tenderness. They craved each other.

"Do you want to go back to my apartment?" Tom asked.

Randall shook his head no and at the same time, pushed his seat all the way back. Tom looked around to double-check that it was deserted up here. Randall's cock pushed against his jeans. That overruled any rational argument Tom was making in his head to leave. The moment was now.

He straddled Randall on the passenger seat. He held onto the handle above the door reserved for parents teaching their kids to drive. Randall met his lips. Tom dragged his fingers through Randall's thick head of hair. He felt the thick sheet of strength pulsing under the sweater. Even wearing a cable-knit sweater Randall still had muscle definition.

The sweater came off. Tom grabbed at those pecs over his sleeveless T-shirt. He grinded into Randall's thick cock, which pressed against his ass. He moaned into Randall's lips at the pressure mounting between them.

Riiiiip

"Shit." He tore the fabric at the top of Randall's sleeveless T-shirt.

"Damn, Tom."

A small tear. It could be sewn up, and Randall probably had plenty more. He and Randall exchanged a look of hungriness. Both were on the same page.

Tom ripped the shirt in half. The sound of fabric ripping was like its own sex noise. And there was that glorious chest, nothing between them. Randall unbuttoned Tom's shirt as Tom's hands figure skated across the smooth skin. Their bare chests met when they kissed again, a bolt of heat on this cold, cold night.

"I have lube," Randall said. He patted one of his pockets under Tom's thigh.

"And magnums?"

He patted the same pocket. "You know it."

Tom wanted to give him an Eagle Scout badge for preparedness. Tom reached behind him to rub the huge mound in Randall's jeans. He couldn't wait for Randall to burrow his length inside that tight hole. Randall let out a grunt of pleasure that swelled Tom's cock even further.

"Wait." Tom opened the passenger door. He dismounted Randall and fell onto the road as gracefully as he could manage.

"What are you doing?"

He got on his knees outside the car and unbuttoned Randall's jeans and pulled down his boxers. That familiar pillar of pleasure shot up in the air.

"Hello, old friend," Tom said. He wanted to make sure that what he saw two weeks ago wasn't a figment of his imagination, some mythical creature that had gotten bigger in his memory.

It. Was. Not.

"Oh tannenbaum, oh tannenbaum," he said. It was not the only thing that Tom liked about Randall. It didn't compare to Randall's caring side, but it was still something Tom could enjoy.

"You going to rock around this Christmas tree or not?" Randall asked, just as quick with the references.

Tom's lips slid down the fireman's pole. Calling it a candy cane would be doing Randall's member a disservice. Randall moaned in his seat. Tom stroked him as he sucked, his hand barely managing to get all the way around his dick.

"Holy shit. Holy shit." Randall's cock filled his mouth completely as Tom took him all the way to the base. His thatch of pubic hair brushed against his lips. Tom came back up for air before he gagged.

"Holy shit," Randall repeated as Tom licked his balls. "That was...holy shit." It was a gold star for Tom. He gave the cock one more suck, for good luck, then rolled on the condom.

He got back in the car and shut the door. Tom pulled

down his pants just below his ass. He realized he should've done this before he got back in the car, but he didn't want to take his pants all the way off in case someone did drive by. He pulled out his cock from the mess of denim just beneath his crotch. The air of the heating vent hit his exposed ass. Randall slipped a lubed finger inside him.

"Fuck." Tom writhed against his finger. He wished he'd stretched before getting in this position, but he was ready. Really ready. He pushed away hair that got in Randall's eyes. The guy was beautiful, but in that moment, Tom saw a different kind of beauty, the kind that radiated from his heart and mind.

Tom rocked back and impaled himself on Randall's thick cock. He bit his lip as it breached his tight ring of muscle. Fuck, it felt good to be filled up like this, completely taken over. He bounced on that cock, his hands pushing against Randall's glistening chest.

"Ride it," Randall grunted out. He slapped Tom's pale ass.

Tom went faster and clenched around his cock. Their eyes connected over the soft light of the radio player and residual light from the houses. Tom loved falling back into Randall's dick. Randall held his hips in place and fucked him, his animal strength in full focus. All those hours spent lifting kids had given him excellent upper arm strength. Randall didn't wince under the weight of Tom on his lap. Another benefit to his rigorous Santa duties.

His cock pounded into Tom's puckered hole. Tom took his hand off the nervous parent handlebar, and stroked himself. He was already close to coming without a hand on himself. Watching Randall's intense face as he thrust inside was such a turn on. Tom rubbed his cock across his sweaty abs for lubrication.

"Fuck." Randall went faster, and Tom tightened around him, waiting for the finish.

"Yeah. You feel so good, Randall."

"We made it through sex without any Christmas puns," Randall said.

"We did." Tom arched back. His cock was so fucking hard and red. He whipped his hand up and down as Randall went balls deep inside him.

"MERRY CHRISTMAS TO ALL AND TO ALL A GOOD NIGHT!" Tom yelled as he sprayed Randall's chest with streaks of come.

Randall shot him an "Anything you can do I can do better" look.

"AND A PARTRIDGE IN A PEAR TREE!" Randall emptied himself into his magnum condom. He pulled out of Tom.

Tom fell back against the glove compartment. He wiped his forehead with the bottom of his opened shirt. "I love the holidays."

CHAPTER 13

Tom had to park in the last row of the parking lot the next morning, but he didn't care. He could've done cartwheels into the mall after the night he had. He had dropped Randall off at his motel early this morning and sang *Twelve Days of Christmas* at the top of his lungs in the car all the way to work.

He laughed to himself at the women crowding into the mall, no doubt going to see Santa. *Well, Santa's taken, sweetheart.* And Tom was taken, taken by guy who continued to surprise him.

Tom waltzed into The Décor Store, put his apron on in the break room, and got onto the floor to help customers. He was assigned to the living room area, which was never too bad unless someone wanted to buy furniture and have it delivered. That was a ghastly amount of paperwork.

Kirsten waited for him in his area, arms folded.

"Dish," she said with restrained calm. Tom knew he owed her some kind of explanation.

"Hi, do you need help with anything?" Tom asked a customer checking out curtain holders.

"No, she doesn't," Kirsten said. "Dish."

"We're on the clock."

"You can't leave me hanging like this. Ma'am." Kirsten turned to the customer, who couldn't be more than twenty-seven. "My co-worker got some last night and is holding back details."

"Let me know if you need help with anything. Vases are twenty percent off." Tom pulled Kirsten to the pillow wall. It was sacred ground. No lying here. "Do you want to get us fired?"

"They won't fire us. We're the best employees here."

She did have a point.

"What is going on with you and Hot Mall Santa? I thought you guys were just friends. Was that a date last night?"

Tom gulped down. Randall said he wasn't in the closet, and Kirsten was one of Tom's closest friends. He couldn't not tell her this. She would do the same.

He nodded yes.

She clamped a pillow over her mouth.

"We have to sell those," he said.

She put back the pillow. Tom turned it so that the part that hit her mouth was against the wall.

"It was a date," he repeated.

"Hot Mall Santa is...of course he is. He's devastatingly attractive."

Tom shrugged a shoulder. She did have a point.

"No wonder he wasn't into my lap dance."

"I'm not sure that could all be pinned on his sexual orientation."

"Have you guys hooked up?"

"We—yeah." Tom tried to keep his voice down.

"So all those times he came into the store to see you, you guys were bumping uglies?"

"I mean, it's not like that, but yeah technically, I guess."

She bit into another pillow. "Holy fuckballs. Oh my Blitzen. You—Tom!"

He worried that her head was going to spin off. He was pretty sure she was excited for him, but there might've been a healthy dose of jealousy on her part.

"You banged Hot Mall Santa! You deserve a monument!"

Tom shushed her, but she waved it off.

"Don't shush me. You got the guy we all wanted. You've had what every person in the South Wing is lusting over."

"I don't think every person..."

She cocked her head at him. She did not have time for this. She did a gimme motion with her hand. "Details, please."

"What?"

"Since I can't get with him, I need to live vicariously through you. You rode on Santa's sleigh. You let him go down your chimney."

"How do you know I didn't go down his chimney?"

"Tom."

Damn her for knowing me so well!

"Tell me everything. How much did you do with him? Did you have sex with Hot Mall Santa?"

"His name is Randall, by the way, and it wasn't just that." Tom didn't want to cheapen what they had. He liked Randall. They had forged a personal connection, one that Tom felt in his heart, even if it was going to end in early January. They shared way more than bodily fluids, but Kirsten didn't seem to have any patience for that stuff.

"Oh, come on. Did he read you French poetry? Or

maybe you guys just kissed. He's probably fucking one of the elves."

A flash of indignant anger hit Tom. "Why would you say that?"

"I don't know." She shrugged. "You're not really a guy into casual sex."

"Yes, I am."

"You're more of a romantic."

"We fucked," Tom said, not letting Kirsten demean his sex appeal. "Oh did we fuck."

He was giving his audience what they wanted.

"Tell me everything."

"His body is like a freaking Greek god, and he had quite a thunderbolt. Like, it's ridiculous. I'm surprised I'm still able to walk. With a body like that, and a sex drive like that, he should be doing porn." Tom couldn't stop. He realized for the first time that having attention showered on you could be addictive. "We fucked all night long. We were in more positions than a sectional sofa. Hot Mall Santa just kept going."

"Holy shit!"

"Oh, yeah. I wore those antlers we had to wear in the store last year. He told me I was on the naughty list."

"He actually said that? That is like a porno."

"I know!" Tom wanted to tell her they were both joking, that it was this amazing kind of sex where they were comfortable enough with each other to laugh and have fun. Right from the start. *Almost like it was meant to be or something.* "His body just overwhelmed. He is like this animal piece of meat. And last night...it was wild. We did it in my car. In public. In a subdivision. He has to use magnum condoms, like for real."

"Shut up!" Kirsten ripped a row of pillows out of the

wall. She immediately put them back, but the thought still stood.

"Hot Mall Santa doesn't fuck around. He is here to play. I didn't know that I could handle him, but..." Tom stopped talking. Kirsten's face changed into one of horror.

Oh crap, there's a customer behind me.

"Is there anything I can help you find to..."

But it wasn't a customer.

Randall.

His body caved in, like Tom had just shot a bunch of arrows at his chest.

"Hey," Tom said, panicking inside.

"I wanted to say hi before I went to the Workshop."

Kirsten waved hello at him, at as much a loss for words as Tom.

"That's what you think of me?" he asked.

"No. No, I don't." Tom looked back at Kirsten, then at him. "We were just joking around."

Kirsten wasn't laughing anymore. Tom wanted to smash his own head into the twenty-percent-off vases.

"Can we talk in private?" Tom asked.

Kirsten left to help a customer, but Randall did not move.

"I have to get to work." Randall's jaw tightened and pain etched across his pretty face. "Last night was really special for me."

"Me, too."

"Then why were you telling Kirsten all those details? You sounded just like the people on line at Santa's Workshop, waiting to give me some line or saying what they want me to do to them."

Why did he have to talk to Kirsten like that? Tom didn't feel that way. But it was safe. It made what he was feeling for

Randall less real, especially when Randall was going to Wisconsin over wherever, probably never to return. "I'm sorry. I never expected someone as hot as you to actually want to be with me."

"So I'm just some hot guy?"

"I didn't mean it that way. But..." Tom knew he should stop, but the words kept coming. "I mean, you *are* hot."

"I thought we'd gotten to know each other over these past few weeks, but I'm still just the Hot Mall Santa to you." Randall took off his Santa hat, where his waves of hair remained voluminous. "Male baldness runs in my family. So if I start to lose my hair, you'll ditch me?"

"No."

"Or what if I get permanently disfigured in an accident?"

"Don't say that."

"I don't want to be with someone who likes me just because of how I look. I'm tired of being just an object. I've tried dating guys before, and that's all they seem to care about. They just wanted to ogle me and show me off. I guess...you're one of them, too."

Tom opened his mouth to say something, but this time, he had no words. He realized that Randall was right. He assumed hot people are shallow, but maybe it was the rest of us who chose to put them in this box. Tom didn't want to be like those other guys, but before he could respond, Randall walked out of the store. People watched him go, wondering if that was the Santa they'd heard so much about.

Tom pulled himself together. Anything he was feeling would have to wait until his lunch break. A customer needed help retrieving a candy dish from the top shelf, and that was his priority. Not the Hot Mall Santa.

CHAPTER 14

One week until Christmas

THE DÉCOR STORE was in a state of controlled chaos. The mad rush was in for procrastinators to get presents on time, but it was nothing Tom couldn't handle. He knew what to expect on this last week of the holidays, and he appreciated the chance to stay so busy.

Hot Mall Santa continued to pack the crowds in. Tom heard of four women thrown out for flashing him and a rumor that a modeling agent had slipped him his card. Tom didn't care if it was true. He did as much as he could to not think about Randall. No more walking past South Wing. No more eating at their not-so-secret lunch spot. Those were givens. But trying to wring Randall out of his mind was proving to be difficult. The things that Tom remembered the most were moments of them talking, of them driving through Veronese Estates, of the way Randall would look at him as if Tom were the most interesting man in the world, and of how Randall was the most interesting person he knew. The guy had been to how many states, and he was hung up on *Tom*? It sounded completely implausible.

Tom had heard another rumor that the mall manager had offered Randall a good chunk of change to come back for Valentine's Day and play mall Cupid. Oakville Mall had never done something like that, but it seemed like a no-brainer. Randall in nothing but a diaper? They'd have money coming out of their ears.

"This can't be happening!" A male customer wearing an ascot yelled at Tom four days before Christmas. "How are you completely out of the cobalt blue decorative spheres? I drove all the way here from Des Moines for them, and now you're saying you don't have them? What am I supposed to do?"

"You drove all the way here from Des Moines, Iowa?" Tom asked.

"Yeah, and you should have decorative spheres!" He didn't seem the least bit concerned about driving five hours to Oakville for literal blue balls.

"I can call up our Des Moines store and see if they have it in stock."

"I don't live in Des Moines." He looked at Tom like he was crazy. "Who cares about Des Moines?"

Seriously?

"I want you to know that I am never shopping at your store again, and I'm going to write a letter to your CEO. He's my cousin. He's going to shut this whole store down and fire you."

"If your cousin is CEO, he could probably track down one of those spheres better than we can."

"He's busy. He's on vacation. He has four kids."

Tom nodded carefully. The CEO of The Décor Store was Margaret Wallis, who had one daughter, if Tom remembered the company newsletter accurately. He liked to joke that his customers were nutty, but then sometimes, they were legit nuts. It was never a dull day in retail.

"You know what? This whole store can lick my asshole." The customer put on sunglasses (it was nighttime) and stalked out.

"Don't you just love the holidays?" Kirsten came over carrying rugs to restock. They frayed and left her apron covered in orange fibers.

"To paraphrase Green Day, wake me up when December ends." Tom took half her rugs and helped her stack them in the rug aisle.

"How are things?" she asked, and she was not talking about customers.

"It's fine."

"Have you gone to see him?"

"Why would I do that? He made it clear he does not want to see me, and it's for the best because he's leaving town. This was just a holiday fling."

Kirsten gave him a hard look. Neither of them believed that.

"Tom, you're taking it awfully rough for it just being a fling."

"You're the one who kept saying that we should all just hook up with Hot Mall Santa because it's the thing to do."

"I did." She placed a rug on the bottom shelf. "And maybe I was wrong."

Kirsten? Admitting she was wrong? Tom must need to clean out his ears.

"Maybe he was something more," she said.

"He wasn't."

"Maybe he was. And maybe you're just scared to admit that."

"Scared?"

"Because you might fail." Kirsten stopped folding and putting rugs back. Now she looked straight at him. "And maybe that will happen, but it doesn't mean you always have to play it safe with your pining and crushing. How awesome were these past few weeks with him?"

Amazing. After his confrontation with Randall, Tom gave her the full scoop. The beach book, the sunscreen, the Wounded Soldier, the presidential audiobook challenge, Veronese Estates. He loved sharing those details more than the ones about sex.

"It doesn't matter now," Tom said.

"I'm sorry for making you say those things about him. I'm so used to objectifying hot guys. I didn't realize they hate that as much as women do."

"I hate to cut this gender studies class short, but we need one of you at the front of the store," Antonio said, peeking his head in.

"I got it," Tom said, grateful for the distance from Kirsten.

———

In retail, spring started right after New Year's. The holiday season was like going on a bender that you wanted to forget as soon as it was over. On top of dealing with the onslaught of holiday shoppers, stores had to prepare their stockrooms for the spring shipments that came in late December. Because of inclement weather downstate, the truck coming with the spring merchandise shipment was delayed, meaning Tom and Antonio and a seasonal worker had to stay late to unload it after closing down the store. The seasonal worker only lasted until 11:15. His curfew was midnight.

The Décor Store felt like a different world during these late nights, one filled with magic and intrigue. Tom used to imagine a *Toy Story*-like scenario where the items all came to life once the customers left. He knew that wasn't real, but it made having to stay here so late a little bit more bearable.

Although Antonio helped with that part, too. He ordered pizza from the Sbarro's before they closed. The box sat on the break room table.

"You got mushrooms?" Tom asked when he flipped the box open.

"I know you love them," Antonio said as he poured himself a cup of coffee.

"Are you okay with them? This is your pizza, too."

"Yep." He sat on the counter, which was probably against corporate policy. Antonio seemed ready to cut loose.

Tom looked at him an extra second. He had had food court pizza for his lunch break several times. He didn't think Antonio ever noticed what kind of pizza he ate.

Tom held up his slice of pizza. "Thanks."

"Let's eat and then get to work." Antonio joined him at the table and took a slice for himself. "I appreciate you staying late, Tom."

"Well, I'm getting paid overtime, so it's all good."

"We really—I really am grateful that you're here. You are this store's secret weapon." An earnestness took hold of the smoldering features of his face, creasing it in ways new to Tom. "Do you remember when we had to do summer inventory—"

"And that display of decanters fell and shattered?"

"Completely shattered! Into a million pieces!"

"We were so exhausted."

"You suggested we put a rug over it rather than clean it up." Antonio broke out laughing.

"I was tired and wanted to go home. Leave me alone!"

Antonio's laughter faded into a smile fixed right for Tom. A wave of chills went up Tom's back. Maybe the smolder wasn't completely gone.

"We've had a lot of good times in this store, Tom." Antonio didn't stop looking at him, like a police officer trying to get his suspect to crack. "I'm glad you're here."

"Yeah." Maybe those dreams he once had of being with Antonio weren't so off-base. Tom needed a glass of water. His hand shook slightly as he poured himself a cup from the watercooler. "We should—we should probably get started."

"You're right. That stockroom is a mess!" Antonio brushed past Tom, his heat pressing on Tom's back. "I'll see you out there."

———

Tom and Antonio got to work organizing the new influxes of boxes in the stockroom. They kept the spring seasonal stock separated from the general evergreen products. Antonio opened some of the spring seasonal boxes to see what new designs the Décor Store would be asking them to sell. Tom focused on keeping the stockroom in a workable condition, but Antonio kept scrambling his circuits. He would find ways to get close to him. Looking over his shoulder to get a look at what Tom was working on. Putting a brief hand on Tom's lower back to maneuver around him when saying "excuse me" would have sufficed. It was all just left of appropriate employee conduct. Perhaps Tom was overanalyzing, but there came a point when enough ambiguous gestures coalesced around a common hypothesis.

I think Antonio is flirting with me.

"A butterfly scented candle." Antonio read the label of the light pink pillar candle. "Flapping Wings."

"How is it?"

"It smells like fresh flowers and cut grass. No butterflies. Why would they name it Flapping Wings?"

"I guess they ran out of spring names for these scents." Many of them smelled the same and were rebranded to seem like new items each year.

"Here. Smell." Antonio put a hand on Tom's back and held Flapping Wings up to Tom's nose. He watched Tom inhale the scent. They were so close Tom smelled him more than the candle.

"It's yeah, grass and flowers. I still like it." Tom's cheeks heated up so much they could've lit Flapping Wings.

Antonio put Flapping Wings back in its box. Out of another one, he pulled a picture frame shaped like an Easter egg. He laughed to himself.

"I can't believe we're going to start putting this stuff on display next week," Antonio said. "Retail moves at the speed of sound."

"It's fun," Tom said. He wasn't one of those people who complained about Christmas stock coming out after Labor Day. "Retail is all about anticipation. You get to look forward to new holidays and new seasons all the time. Anticipation is the best part."

"What about the actual holiday?"

"Can't live up to the anticipation." Tom shrugged his shoulders, like that was his story and he was sticking to it despite feeling very nervous for some reason that he didn't want to think about.

They continued moving around boxes and getting the stockroom in order. There were cubby areas for different types of stock which corresponded to sections in the store, an organization Tom made sure his fellow employees stuck to. He had to direct Antonio to the proper section for boxes he carried.

"You are a paragon, Tom." Antonio rubbed his arm with his firm hand. If hands could smolder...but Tom would rather have the tender touch of Randall.

They took a break shortly thereafter for another slice of pizza and some water and coffee. Tom's throat got that scratchy feeling when he stayed up late. Fortunately, he wasn't opening tomorrow so he could sleep in.

"I'm sorry things didn't work out with you and the Santa guy," Antonio said.

Tom shrugged it off, feeling weird discussing this aspect of his personal life.

"It's his loss."

"I guess," Tom said.

"It is," Antonio said with conviction. "It's his loss for not seeing what a wonderful, thoughtful, sharp guy you are."

He wasn't used to compliments and focused on his pizza. And he couldn't get over the feeling that Antonio was flirting with him. Majorly flirting. Throughout their relationship, it was just Tom wishing and hoping and nothing happening. What changed?

"I've always known who you are." Antonio looked at him with those intense eyes again. "I know I've said it a million times, but I don't know what I'd do without you here."

Something snapped inside Tom. Inside of swooning at such a nice compliment, it fired him up. *If I'm so important to you, then why have I not been promoted?*

Antonio was definitely flirting with him, but why now?

And then Tom had his answer.

Hot Mall Santa.

"You okay, Tom? You have this weird look. Cute, but weird."

Cute. Antonio's smoldering words were nails on a chalkboard to Tom now.

"I started to think that you were into me. You've been flirting with me all night, more than usual."

"What? Tom, I think you have the wrong idea..."

"Oh, I do." Tom put down the box of picture frames. He was hit with a sucker punch of clarity. "I am such an idiot. Such an idiot. You were never into me. You only flirted so that I would take shifts nobody else wanted or not complain about getting passed over for a promotion.

"I have had the wrong idea this whole time. You were jealous of Randall, not because he was with me, but because he took the attention away from you, because suddenly you weren't the center of my universe."

Tom listened to himself clearly for the first time. He couldn't believe he had been into this guy. He had had a retail mindset of only wanting the anticipation. But Randall was the holiday. When he was with Randall, there was no pining. Only living.

"I can't even blame you. I let this happen. I let myself have this hopeless crush on you because it was safe. Nothing will ever happen between us, so I never had to worry about being rejected or hurt. And you strung me along just enough."

"I think you should go home and get some sleep. You're not thinking clearly. I think you're overworked."

"You're never leaving Milo."

"Tom..."

"And I'm never getting promoted."

"I told you. I'm working on that. These things take time. If I could promote you right this second, I would."

"Antonio, cut the shit. Has corporate given any reason why I haven't been promoted? I do all the things an assistant manager does already." Another bolt of clarity hit Tom. "Why would you need to promote me? I do all the work of an assistant manager at a sales associate wage. I make you look so good."

"Tom, take a walk outside. Get some fresh air."

Tom saw that smolder for what it really was. Manipulation. He laughed to himself. His pining had completely screwed over his job prospects.

"I quit," Tom said. "I'm going to find myself a manager position."

"Those jobs don't grow on trees. You're going to give up this path that we're carving for you here?"

"I am." Tom breathed in stale stockroom air that refreshed his lungs as if he were hiking in the woods. "But not tonight. I'm not a dick. I'm giving my two weeks notice."

Tom got back to work. As luck would have it, he made his declaration at midnight. It was a new day, and a new world for Tom. He was ready for more risk. Tis the season, right?

CHAPTER 15

Christmas Eve

TOM SIGNED up for the last available slot of the night to see Santa. He waited with the rest of the 5:30 group in the line that snaked through South Wing. Tom remembered coming to see Santa as a little kid with his mom. He was never impressed. He would make awkward small talk with Santa without giving his wish list. She had been open with him about who really made gifts appear, and it wasn't some random dude up at the North Pole. His mom worked hard to buy her son Christmas gifts, and she deserved the credit.

Randall seemed like a Santa natural, despite not having the body type one would expect. Even though most people who sat on his lap were there not out of the holiday spirit, he put on his best Santa show, staying committed to the role. He asked them what they wanted for Christmas and side-stepped any come-ons. Tom recognized the buoyant energy of his voice from their conversations in their not-so-secret hiding spot and that night at The Wounded Soldier. "Ho Ho Ho" bellowed throughout the workshop.

Tom had spent his morning perusing job boards for any manager positions. It was pretty quiet on the job front, but he knew retail, and more positions would open up in January. People rode out the holiday season before moving around.

Kirsten had screamed out *YES!* when he told her the news. He knew Kirsten was a full volume person, but her reaction still surprised him. He gave her the international *keep it down* signal, since they were both on duty.

"I'm so happy for you," she said.

"You are? I quit, and I don't have another job lined up." The reality hit Tom when he woke up. Any surge of excitement he had felt when he told Antonio had been smoothed down by a gust of fear.

"You're betting on yourself."

He liked how she put it. "I'm scared."

"That's natural. It's good to be a little scared. Keeps things interesting."

"Can you please not congregate?" Antonio said curtly. "We have customers that need to be attended to." He only looked at Kirsten, then walked away.

She glanced at Tom, who acknowledged the awkwardness.

"On break, I'm going to want details," she said.

Tom was next in line. Randall was mere feet from him, in all his Santa glory. Most customers didn't take the time to notice the care and consideration Randall put into his job. Tom felt bad for them. Sure, they'd get to ogle his body, but they had no idea they were missing out on discovering his sense of humor, thoughtfulness, and a mind filled with fascinating historical facts. There was so much else he wanted to share with Randall besides sex.

"Do you know what you're going to ask Santa for?" the elf asked him.

"Yes."

"Good. It helps the line move faster."

Tom was a little scared now. No, a lot scared. But Kirsten was right. It was good to be scared. Scared meant he was moving in the right direction.

The rope clinked open. Santa's lap awaited.

Tom couldn't make out Randall's reaction to him because of the full Santa beard covering his face. *Santa wouldn't throw somebody off his lap, would he?*

He took tentative steps forward. He remembered how the Santa suit scratched against his skin, how Randall probably had on a sleeveless T-shirt underneath.

"Hi," Tom said.

"Hey," Randall said uneasily.

"May I?" Tom pointed at his lap. "I don't have to if—"

"Yeah. Sure. That's why you waited in line."

"Right." Tom stood between his thighs and double-checked with Randall before lowering himself onto his lap. "Let me know if I'm too heavy for you. I don't want to cut off your blood circulation."

"You're not." Randall let out a short laugh. Tom wasn't sure what was so funny until he remembered that he'd straddled Randall in his car. So yeah, Randall could handle him.

"Did you know that Franklin Pierce was the first president to have a Christmas tree installed in the White House?"

"I did know that," Randall said.

"Oh."

"So what would you like for Christmas?" he asked without much enthusiasm.

"I'm not a very materialistic person, but I gave it a lot of thought." Tom's chest vibrated with nerves. The fear rose up through his body, threatened to shut him down, but he powered through it. "I want you, Randall. I want you back. I might not have you for much longer, but I want us to spend whatever time you have left in Oakville together." The fear tried taking over his mouth, tying his tongue down and cuffing his vocal chords, but Tom refused to stay quiet. "I didn't mean what I said about you. I was scared that I actually liked you, because guys like you don't usually go for guys like me."

"Hot guys?"

"*Good* guys," Tom said with emotion. "Guys who leave notes under drawers and actually plan out dates. Guys who I can't wait to talk to when my shift is over and who treat idiots like me so well even though we probably don't deserve it. *That's* what makes you sexy."

Randall remained stoic. His Santa beard hid his facial expressions.

"So you want me for Christmas?" Randall asked.

"Yes."

"And after Christmas?"

Tom nodded. A simple yes would not suffice. Not even Kirsten's screaming yes would.

"Even if I was permanently disfigured?"

"Yes. As long as there's no blood. I'm queasy around blood."

Tom pulled down Randall's beard, where a big smile waited for him. He leaned in, wondering if Randall would lean, too. Their lips met and made Tom whole again.

"Hey! Hey!" The security guard ran over and yanked

Tom off of him. "No kissing Santa! How many times do we have to tell patrons?"

"It's okay," Randall said to the guard. He turned to Tom. "This is not the first time someone has tried to put the moves on Santa this season."

"I wasn't putting the moves on Santa. We were reconciling," Tom explained to the guard. "And in my defense, I didn't use tongue."

"No hanky-panky with Santa!" the guard said, not amused.

Too late for that.

The guard led Tom away from Santa's Workshop.

"Wait!" he heard Randall yell.

Randall caught up to them. He kissed Tom on the cheek. "Maybe you can give me a ride home tonight?"

Tom couldn't stop grinning.

CHAPTER 16

Christmas Day

TOM AND RANDALL had gone back to Tom's apartment last night once Randall's final Santa shift was over. They talked a little bit more about what happened, but then Randall suggested they watch *Die Hard*, and things quickly escalated. Tom broke out the antlers again.

They awoke the next morning, Tom in Randall's muscular arms, his biceps squeezing against Tom's chest, his morning wood digging into Tom's ass.

Merry Christmas, indeed.

"Good morning, Santa," Tom said. He dangled a finger through Randall's messy hair.

"You can't call me that anymore." Randall's eyes squinted open. His raised his arm to block out the sun. "I'm officially no longer Santa Claus."

"The mystery is over. You're just regular now. Bummer."

Randall cocked an eyebrow.

"How does it feel to no longer be Santa?" Tom asked.

"I won't miss the costume. That's for sure."

That led to an awkward silence, not out of memory of the costume, but about what happened next. Randall's time in Oakville was coming to an end, something Tom was always aware of, but it hit him extra hard now. When he was in the thick of the holiday season, Tom didn't think much of life post-Christmas. It was in this foggy future that seemed far off, like retirement. *Oh, come January 2nd, I'm going to get my life back on track and learn five new languages...*

But January was closer than ever now.

"So Wisconsin next, right?" Tom asked. "Do you have another job lined up?"

"Not yet. I may wise up and go someplace warmer. Wisconsin in January is probably not ideal."

"Yeah. That's smart." Tom got a lump in his throat thinking about Randall moving to some warm, far-flung location. "What do you want to do?"

"I don't know. Maybe there's a farm I could work on, or I can work at a luxury resort setting out lounge chairs."

"What do you want to do, though?" Tom asked. He thought about the track he had been on at The Décor Store, and he wondered if Randall wanted anything like that. Some people weren't meant for structure. "Do you want a career or anything long-term?"

Randall's brow creased with gorgeous lines of thought. "I don't know. It wasn't something I'd thought about when I was younger. And then I started traveling, and I focused on finding jobs that could pay my way."

"If you could do anything, what would it be?"

The lines on Randall's forehead creased in thought. It wasn't an easy question. Tom knew he was fortunate. He figured out retail was the career for him at a young age. Not everyone was that lucky.

Randall's phone dinged with the sound of an email. He immediately groaned when he saw the subject line.

"A last minute Dear Santa letter?" Tom asked.

"This guy wants me to be a model. He got my information from my boss."

An idea clicked into Tom's head. He sat up in bed. "Why don't you?"

He could already sense Randall's objection, but kept going.

"I know. You don't want to be used for your body. But models can make good money. Maybe you model for a little bit and save up some money until you figure out what you want to do." Tom kneeled beside Randall, energy flowing through him. "Lots of people have done that. There are people who strip to pay for law school and the actors who take roles in dumb blockbusters so they can work on small, personal films for no money."

He saw the wheels turning in Randall's head. He didn't know where modeling would take Randall. Perhaps all around the world. They might not see each other again, but if it meant Randall could have a future where he would be happy and fulfilled, it would be worth it. Maybe they were only meant to be a Christmas fling. Maybe they came into each other's lives for a specific reason.

"At least hear the guy out. If he sounds shady or you don't like what he has planned for you, you can say no."

"You're right." Randall shielded his face from the sun, which was cutting with extra strength through the window. He got out of bed to close the blinds, his pert, firm ass on full display. It made Tom's mouth practically water.

Tom jumped out of bed and slapped his butt. Since their time was probably coming to an end, he had better make the most of it.

"What was that for?" Randall asked, smirking.

"Just because."

"Oh yeah?" Randall turned Tom around and slapped his naked ass back. "How do you like that?"

"I hated it. Do it again."

He slapped it again with extra force. Randall pulled Tom against him, and his thick cock pressed against Tom's opening.

"Santa, I thought you'd be so worn out from traveling around the world last night."

"You'd be amazed at my stamina." He slapped Tom's ass again.

Tom let out a loud moan. He neighbors were away for the holidays, so he didn't try to restrain himself. Randall kissed along his neck, tender kisses laced with lust. He grabbed Tom's chest and palmed his hard cock. Tom found himself bending forward and holding onto the blinds.

"So greedy. Santa just saw you last night," Randall said. He opened Tom's cheeks and spat inside. He thwacked his heavy cock against Tom's raw hole.

And then he left.

"Randall?" Tom heard a commotion in the living room. He went to go check it out, and Randall appeared in the doorway holding the string of lights from his Christmas tree.

"You won't be needing these anymore this season, right?" Randall held up the lights in his hand.

Tom shook his head no.

"Good. Because somebody's being greedy with Santa. And somebody needs to learn a lesson." Randall wrapped the lights around Tom's chest and arms. These lights were non-toxic and safe for children to chew, so Tom wasn't worried. Just turned on.

He tried moving his arms to no avail.

"What are you going to do, Santa?"

Tom's cock was ridiculously hard. Randall quirked a dangerous eyebrow at him and used the rest of the lights as a leash and led Tom to the edge of the bed. He pushed Tom down so that his ass had no choice but to stick straight in the air, defenseless against whatever Randall wanted to do with it.

Randall plugged in the lights. Tom's body lit up. With the blinds closed, the lights twinkled extra bright.

"Fuck me, Santa," Tom said. "I mean, Randall."

Randall got close to his ear. Tom could feel the ball of the Santa hat bouncing on his shoulder. "It's technically Christmas, so I'll let you have one more day with Santa."

He pushed Tom down so his face was mashed against the bed. Moments later, he slid two slicked-up fingers inside Tom, and then came the magnum opus, so to speak.

Tom cried out in want, and a little pain, as Randall entered him. He pulled on the Christmas lights as a bridle. Tom felt himself stretch to fit all of Santa. Randall pulled him by the hips. There was no going slow this time around. They were all passion. Tom's legs buckled under the weight of Randall's impact.

Randall yanked him up so they could both look at each other through the mirror above Tom's bed. The lights pressed into Tom's skin like pinches, but damn if he didn't look hot being completely controlled by Randall in his Santa hat. Randall wrapped his hand around Tom's cock and stroked him while banging into his pink opening.

"You didn't leave any milk and cookies for Santa last night," Randall said. "Big fucking mistake."

"Teach me my lesson, Santa."

They both smiled at this fun banter. It was the best way

to burn off the stress of the holidays. And damn if it wasn't hot hearing those lines come from Randall's husky, strangled breath.

Randall pulled him against his massive erection, making Tom take him to the base. He squeezed both of Tom's nipples, then one hand returned to the bridle and the other wrapped around Tom's straining cock. His balls drew up, and his heart was going to explode out of his chest.

"Fuck. This feels so good. I mean, it doesn't because I'm being punished for...for something. Fuck." He shot his load across his bedspread. Streak after streak as Tom emptied himself completely. He collapsed face-first since his arms were tied and his legs were pretty much useless.

"Tom! Are you okay?" Randall flipped him over.

"Yeah. You wore me out."

Randall re-entered him with Tom on his back. Now Tom could watch his expression that he loved so much. The pained orgasm face. Randall's cock tore through his ass. Even though he was spent, he still felt immense pleasure from his heavy thrusts.

"Tom...Tom..." Randall said as he came, his eyes in a fog. It was sexier than any Christmas pun.

He lay next to Tom and caught his breath.

"Merry..." Randall began.

Tom kissed him quiet. "Enough holiday talk."

———

TOM INVITED Randall to his mom's for Christmas dinner. Randall couldn't wait.

"It's just dinner. There isn't anything that Christmas-y about it. It's like a back-up Thanksgiving."

"My family didn't celebrate either holiday, so I'll take it!" He beamed an infectious smile. It was the little things.

After they got showered, Tom drove Randall back to his motel so he could change out of his Santa clothes. Randall packed a bag with another change of clothes since he'd probably be spending the night with Tom again. While Tom waited for Randall to get dressed, he got a call on his phone from an unknown number. The area code looked familiar, but he couldn't place it at the moment.

"I'm going outside to take this," Tom told Randall.

It was a warmer than usual Christmas day, with the air slightly balmy, like one of those days better suited to the end of February. The remaining blotches of snow on the ground looked like people who refused to leave a party after it ended.

"Hello?" Tom answered.

"Tom. This is Jordan Benkendorf at The Décor Store corporate."

"Um, hi." Tom wished Randall was out there with him so he could shoot him the biggest WTF look ever. Tom had met Jordan multiple times whenever he came to visit their store. He was the regional manager, Antonio's boss, and would do regular checks.

"I am so sorry to call you on Christmas Day. I will make this brief. I wanted to get in touch with you as soon as I heard the news."

"What news?"

"That...I heard you resigned from The Décor Store recently."

"I did." He had so many WTF looks for Randall. He sat on the curb where his car was. He didn't care that it was a little wet and sopped through his pants. "I didn't know sales associates resigning was news."

"Usually, it's not. But frankly, you're not a regular sales associate. I've been watching you these past three years. Your annual manager and peer reviews have been outstanding. The mystery shoppers we employ have sung your praises, too." *So they do have mystery shoppers!* Tom and Kirsten believed that was just urban legend, a veiled threat managers use to warn employees against treating customers poorly. "Traffic has increased considerably at the Oakville location, and we want to keep you in the fold."

This also sounded like an urban legend, a retail store fighting to keep one of its Regular Joe employees. Tom wasn't going to blow this opportunity. "If you think I'm so great, then why have I not been promoted to assistant manager? I do the work of one."

"We wanted to a few months ago, but Antonio said he spoke to you, and that you weren't interested. He said you were planning to quit to go back to school."

"What? That's not true!"

"I know it's not. I ran into Kirsten at a Christmas Eve party. My new girlfriend happens to be her cousin, and trust me, she let me know that wasn't true."

Tom's head spun with a million questions. "I've wanted to get promoted for so long. He knew that. I don't understand...why would he do that?"

"I don't know. But I'm going to have a meeting with him next week."

Antonio wasn't into Tom. He knew that for sure. *But he just wants me under his thumb. He wants to be admired.* Everything Randall couldn't stand about being Hot Mall Santa Antonio desired. Tom was going to be sick.

"I don't want to work with Antonio ever again."

"I understand. Bottom line, Tom. The Décor Store believes strongly in promoting from within and keeping good employees in the fold. We would like you to stay. The next assistant manager position that opens up in the area, I'm going to recommend you for. Would you be willing to relocate?"

Tom looked at the closed motel room door. He thought of all the risks that awaited him. Randall opened the door, looking as handsome as Tom ever saw him in a cranberry sweater and jeans.

"Tom?" Jordan said through the phone.

But his smile. That hit right at Tom's heart. He knew this was not just a holiday fling.

CHAPTER 17

Eleven Months Later (a.k.a. Five weeks until Christmas again)

EILEEN NEEDED THIS WREATH. Pine needles curled in a tight, welcoming circle with pinecones dotting the edges. It was the wreath for people who wanted to celebrate the "holiday season" instead of Christmas. Tastefully nondescript was what Tom would call it.

And tastefully nicked, too. Eileen pointed to small chips on the wicker edges of the wreath.

"Do you see that?" She put her finger on a microscopic mark that Tom needed a magnifying glass to see. "It's all scuffed up. Which is a shame because it's so pretty."

He knew her game. She was not the first customer to point out a teeny-tiny flaw in order to get a discount. Tom once had a customer purchase $1,500 worth of damaged merchandise—some of it legit damaged—for the discount.

"I am sorry about that. It happens. These products are shipped from warehouses and moved to our stockrooms, then put out here. We do our very best to ensure that they stay in perfect condition, but on rare occasions, things happen. You can always order a new one online. I believe The Décor Store is running a special sale for Cyber Monday this year."

"I can't wait for that. We're having people over for Thanksgiving tomorrow."

"We don't have any extras in the stockroom. I checked," said Donna. She was a plump forty-something mother of two who ironed her employee apron before her shifts. Tom knew if Donna said she checked, he didn't have to second-guess her.

"Are you sure?" Eileen asked.

"We are," Tom said.

Eileen ran her hand across the wreath, stopping on the mark like she was trying to stop the blood flow in a bullet wound. "It's a really nice wreath..."

"If you are willing to take it as is, I can offer ten percent off," Tom said.

"It is all scuffed up. I think twenty percent might be more appropriate."

Ha! What planet are you living on, Eileen? This woman had much to learn.

"Unfortunately, I'm not authorized to give that kind of discount."

"Can I speak to a manager then?" Eileen asked.

"I *am* the manager," Tom said. That sentence never got old to him. "I can call around to other stores, see if they might have it. Or like I said, you can order it online."

Tom smiled his most customer-friendly smile, which told her she was losing this game of chicken.

"I'll take this one," she said quietly, defeated. "With the ten percent," she added with her last gasp.

"Wonderful. I love this wreath. Donna can bring this to the register for you."

"Be careful," the woman said as Donna lifted.

"Donna will take excellent care of it," Tom said.

"I will, like it's one of my own children."

Eileen walked up to the register, with Donna behind her. Donna turned around and shot Tom a knowing smile. He gave her a nod of solidarity. Like any good manager, he had her back.

Tom strolled through his bustling store. His associates diligently helped customers and cleaned up their zones and completed transactions. After only six months as an assistant manager, Tom was promoted to manager. Like he had told Jordan on the phone almost a year ago, he'd been given the work of an assistant manager for a while, just without the title. When given the opportunity to be a true ass man, Tom ran with it.

The pillow wall was on the verge of having a pillow mudslide. The row of festive throw pillows were jammed to one side and slowly spilling onto the floor, while larger pillows were laid flat rather than sitting up and sticking out on their side. He didn't blame his employees. Most customers never put merchandise back the way it should go.

He fixed up the wall, organizing the pillows by size and color. It wasn't until he turned around did he realize he had an audience.

"Nice job," Randall said. He wore mesh shorts and a tank top with his guns proudly displayed. Sunglasses perched atop his head. It had been his uniform lately.

"How's the weather outside?"

"Still sunny and gorgeous. This is Florida. The beautiful weather isn't going away anytime soon, Tom."

Some days, Tom would wake up thinking he was back in

Oakville and that he would be facing a cold, gray day—and Antonio. But then he would open his window, breathe in that warm ocean air, and thank his lucky stars that there'd been an assistant manager position open in Florida.

Antonio had resigned from The Décor Store shortly after Christmas. No store in the Oakville Mall would hire him. Last Tom heard, he was working as a sales associate at a Discount Barn Outlet.

Every morning, Tom stood on his back porch, which looked out on the ocean, and drank his coffee. Sunlight sparkled on the water. The blue of the ocean didn't seem real to him. It was like Florida had discovered Photoshop for physical objects. Randall would join him, kissing his shoulder to let him know he was there. Tom needed those soft kisses like his morning coffee. He couldn't believe this was his life.

Tom missed his mom and Kirsten, but both were happy to have a free place to stay in a warm climate. When he first moved down, his mom came with him to help him settle into his new apartment. They treated it as the Florida vacation they always planned to go on, with plenty of beach time. In fact, both ladies had flown down to celebrate Thanksgiving with him and Randall. They planned to take his mom and Kirsten to lunch at the News Café this weekend for prime people watching. Randall was planning to invite his cousin and aunt down for Christmas. He'd gotten back in touch with his parents, who still did not approve of his sexual orientation or that he dressed up as Santa, but they still wished him well. It was a baby step, and Randall hoped the first of many.

By the pillow wall, Randall slipped his arms around Tom's waist, which Tom pushed off.

"I'm on duty."

"And you're drop dead sexy at it."

"I have to make an example of myself for my employees."

Randall cupped Tom's ass and gave it a slap. "Was that a bad example?"

Fortunately, Tom's apron covered the tightening in his pants.

"Or was fucking your boyfriend in the break room a bad example?"

Tom shushed him, maybe a bit too loud since a customer looked over. "Do you need help with anything? I love those baskets. I use them for extra umbrellas."

"Good idea," the customer said.

Tom turned back to his boyfriend. "Please do not mention that again while I'm working. Even though it was really good."

He whispered the last part just to be safe. That had been an amazing night, and the break room table had proven remarkably stable.

"Do you need me to pick up anything from the grocery store?" Randall asked.

"No. Mom and Kirsten said they're cooking Thanksgiving dinner as a thank you for letting them crash at our apartment."

"Perfect. So all we have to do is eat." Randall leaned on an outdoor table display. His biceps flexed under his weight. This tank top made his muscles seem larger than usual. Randall caught him looking.

"I was looking at your soul," Tom said.

"Right."

Michelle, one of the seasonal employees, came up to Randall with something familiar hanging out of her apron's front pocket.

"Tom, I'm technically not on duty for another three minutes," she said quickly. "Is this your boyfriend?"

"It is. I hope you brought your own Sharpie."

Michelle produced said marker in her hand. Tom motioned for her to go ahead. Randall pulled the calendar out of her front pocket.

"Sorry," she said. "I do love your calendar so much. Could you make it out to Arnold. That's my brother."

"Which month?" Randall asked.

She flipped to June, which for Flag Day, Randall waved a miniature (though not that miniature) flag in front of his dick.

Randall scribbled his name just to the right of his abs. He had signed with the modeling agent who had contacted him in his Hot Mall Santa days. To capitalize on his viral fame, they put together a calendar with Randall celebrating a different holiday nude each month. At first, Randall didn't know if he wanted himself to be this kind of famous. Tom was supportive either way. He wasn't recognized that often, only by people Tom worked with and some guys at the bars. It wasn't like sitting on a throne being ogled every single day. And the money was much, much better. He had gone to New York for the photo shoot for a few weeks last winter. He and Tom had kept up talking and texting, and he returned to Oakville when he was done, renting a room from Kirsten's college friend. Tom would never forget that day when he came back. Randall wanted to be with him, and he couldn't deny that he wanted to be with Randall.

When Tom had heard about an open assistant manager position in Miami last March, he decided to take a risk and apply for a transfer. Randall not only supported him, but came along. He could model from anywhere, and with the money he was earning, he had enrolled in history classes at a local college once they moved down. He had his sights set on going to law school. "I really will be like those guys who strip to pay for law school," he had said during one evening stroll along the beach, holding hands with Tom. "Except, you know, modeling."

"Which is a classier version of stripping," Tom joked.

Randall handed back the calendar and the sharpie to Michelle. She scurried back to the break room to put them in her locker.

His arms returned around Tom's waist and planted a luscious kiss on Tom's lips, one that was quick but said all it needed to say.

"Okay, now I'll leave you alone," Randall said.

Tom kissed him back. "Good. Because this is very unprofessional." He walked with Randall to the store entrance. "I'll see you at home."

"Awesome. I love you," Randall said.

"I love you, too." Those words were still new for Tom, and each time he heard them was like finding another present under the Christmas tree.

Randall left, and Tom thought of him as he straightened out the throw pillows on a sofa in the front window.

"Oh. My. Lord," Donna said, her eyes fixed on something outside. This Décor Store location wasn't inside a mall, but in a downtown promenade that looked out on a busy street. The location filled the store with sunlight.

"What is it?" Tom asked.

"There's a guy walking down the street wearing a Santa hat and a red thong." Donna giggled like a schoolgirl. Other women came over to ogle the man.

"That is one hot Santa," Michelle said.

Tom peeked out the window. "I've seen hotter."

THE END

Want to read a spicy bonus epilogue between Tom and Randall? If you're a fan of people having sex up against windows, then Merry Christmas and Happy Hanukkah to you!

Sign up for my newsletter The Outsiders and start reading this scene as well as all my other freebies today. Grab the Hot Mall Santa bonus scene.

Outsiders always get the first scoop on my new titles, new covers, and sneak peeks, plus members-only contests and other cool goodies via my newsletter. Get in with the Out crowd today at www.ajtruman.com/outsiders.

Please consider leaving a review where you got this book or on Goodreads. Reviews are crucial in helping other readers find new books.

Join the party in my Facebook Group and on Instagram @ajtruman_author. Follow me at Bookbub to be alerted to new releases.

And then there's email. I love hearing from readers! Send me a note anytime at info@ajtruman.com. I always respond.

ALSO BY A.J. TRUMAN

If you're looking for funny, steamy, low-angst stories about small town cuties or college guys, you've come to the right place.

Please visit www.ajtruman.com to learn more about each of my series.

South Rock High

Ancient History

Drama!

Romance Languages

Advanced Chemistry

Single Dads Club

The Falcon and the Foe

The Mayor and the Mystery Man

The Barkeep and the Bro

Browerton University Series

Out in the Open

Out on a Limb

Out of My Mind

Out for the Night

Out of This World

Outside Looking In

Out of Bounds

Seasonal Novellas

Fall for You

You Got Scrooged

Hot Mall Santa

Only One Coffin

ABOUT THE AUTHOR

A.J. Truman writes books with **humor, heart, and hot guys.** What else does a story need? He lives in a very full house in Indiana with his husband, son, and fur babies. He loves happily ever afters and sneaking off for an afternoon movie.

www.ajtruman.com
info@ajtruman.com
The Outsiders - Facebook Group

Printed in Great Britain
by Amazon

32975062R00081